HEARTBREAK HILL

"How about taking a break from your run, Maureen?" Jake offered. "Sit down with us and watch the ducks." A small boy nearby was tossing breadcrumbs into the water, where about fifty ducks quacked hungrily.

Maureen noticed there were glints of red and gold in his thick brown hair. She loved the way it was blown back from his face by the wind. Jake's eyes were warm and inviting, and for a moment she wavered and then felt herself start toward the bench.

But no! What was she doing? Here she was, all hot and sweaty, dressed in her worst-looking sweatshirt and shorts. She probably looked awful, she didn't even know him—what would they talk about? The ducks?

Flustered and embarrassed, Maureen backed up onto the jogging path. She was going to blow it, she knew. But she just couldn't help herself. "Sorry, I—I can't stop jogging in the middle of a run. I'm—I'm in training. Got to go."

Bantam Sweet Dreams Romances
Ask your bookseller for the books you have missed

Heartbreak Hill

Carol Macbain

BANTAM BOOKS

TORONTO · NEW YORK · LONDON · SYDNEY · AUCKLAND

RL 6, IL age 11 and up

HEARTBREAK HILL
A Bantam Book / January 1987

ISBN 0-553-26195-9

Published simultaneously in the United States and Canada

Bantam Books are published by Bantam Books, Inc. Its trademark,
consisting of the words "Bantam Books" and the portrayal of
a rooster, is Registered in U.S. Patent and Trademark Office
and in other countries. Marca Registrada. Bantam Books, Inc.,
666 Fifth Avenue, New York, New York 10103.

PRINTED IN THE UNITED STATES OF AMERICA

O   0 9 8 7 6 5 4 3 2 1

Heartbreak Hill

One

"Hey, look, Debbie. There's the lead runner! Here he comes!"

Maureen clapped her hands hard, filled with excitement as the first runner crested Heartbreak Hill. Fresh cheers and a wave of applause preceded the solitary figure as the waiting crowd caught sight of him and the police escort that was clearing a path for the front runners. Both girls clapped with all their strength and cheered as the long-legged, sweat-drenched number one hundred fourteen ran toward them. His gait was still fast and steady. Only the glassy stare of his eyes revealed that he had only a few more miles to complete the twenty-six grueling miles of the Boston Marathon.

As the runner approached, a tall, angular boy loaded down with cameras pushed past the two girls and darted into the street. He took some head-on shots of the approaching runner, deftly stepping aside at the last minute. Maureen was

1

so impressed by the confident, professional way he handled his cameras, changing lenses and switching settings quickly, that she almost forgot to get a glimpse of the runner as he sped past her.

All of a sudden the boy swung around and took a close-up of Debbie and Maureen in the crowd. Taken by surprise, Maureen was caught staring. Smiling, she brushed a wisp of blond hair back from her forehead after he took his camera down from his eye.

"Hi, Debbie," he said casually. "Want to be in the paper? I need some crowd shots to go along with my marathon coverage."

"Sure, why not? You should have warned us, though. I think I blinked."

The boy smiled, and to Maureen it was as if the sun had suddenly come out. She had never seen anyone with such a dazzling smile.

"No, you didn't," he replied. "I like candids, anyway. You two looked like you were having a good time. Great race, isn't it? This guy is so fast he might break the world record." He paused. "Make sure you check the *Gazette* this week. Maybe you'll be in it."

"I better *not* be if my eyes are closed," Debbie retorted.

"Don't worry. You'll look great!"

"Is that a promise?"

"Absolutely."

What was it about him that appealed to her so strongly? Maureen wondered. She watched him as he joked with Debbie. He looked too young to be working as a professional for a newspaper, she thought, but he acted as if he had a serious assignment. He held one camera ready to shoot, another was slung over one shoulder, and a heavy bag of lenses was strapped across the opposite shoulder. The leather bands crisscrossed his chest, giving him the look of a Mexican bandit—minus the drooping black moustache, of course.

"You look pretty snazzy yourself. Here, let me take a picture of you," Debbie offered, reaching for his Nikon. "Uh-oh. I don't exactly know how to work this. Here, Maureen, you do it."

She slipped the strap around Maureen's neck.

"Don't worry, it's all set. Just shoot. Everything else is automatic," the boy offered.

Maureen felt someone jostle her elbow. Remembering that she was in a large crowd of people, she stepped out into the street and held the camera up to her eye. The boy lounged against a parking meter for his portrait and smiled just as the shutter clicked.

"Hey, thanks," he said, coming over to where she stood. "You know, I have practically no pictures of myself. Ever since I was old enough to hold a camera, I've taken all the pictures in my family, so I end up not being in any." He looked

3

at Maureen for a moment before reaching for his camera, and she felt her face flush. Then he smiled and turned to wink at Debbie. "Well, got to get back to work. See you guys later."

He quickly crossed the street, turning to wave at the girls before disappearing into the crowd on the other side.

Maureen stood quietly, lost in thought. For some reason, her heart was pounding, and all she wanted to do was to relive those last few seconds when he'd looked at her and smiled and then taken the camera from her hands. Darn it. Why couldn't she joke around easily with boys the way Debbie did? She hoped the picture would turn out OK. Maybe he'd remember her then.

A burst of applause and cheering and a nudge from Debbie announced the arrival of the second runner over the hill.

"How do you get to know so many cute boys?" Maureen asked as the runner passed by and the cheers subsided.

"Well, I guess because I've lived here all my life," Debbie responded. "I've known a lot of the kids we go to school with since grade school. It must be hard to move to a new town the way you did just before high school."

"You could at least have introduced me!"

Astonished, Debbie turned to look at her friend. "I'm sorry, Mo. I thought everybody knew

4

Jake. He's a photographer for the yearbook. You can't help running into him. He covers everything. He's always getting photos of school events published in the town paper."

"I wouldn't mind having the photo I took. Those eyes . . ."

"Yeah, he's cute, isn't he? A boy doesn't deserve eyes like that. Those long dark lashes are too irresistible."

"You're right."

"You know, Maureen, you look a little shell-shocked." Debbie giggled. "It's about time you found yourself a boyfriend. It would be fun to go on double dates."

"Oh, come on. Now you sound like my relatives. 'Maureen, you're so pretty. When are you going to find a boyfriend?' " she mimicked. "Even my mom seems disappointed that I'm not very popular."

"But you *are* popular. The kids like you a lot."

"Sure, they *like* me. But the guys don't want to take me out. This is my second year at Coolidge High, and I haven't had a single date."

"Maybe if you were around more on weekends, they'd realize you were available. Out of sight, out of mind, you know. You never go to the games or the pool, you don't hang out at the Ice Cream Corner. . . . Everyone probably thinks you have a secret boyfriend in college."

5

"But I like to see my dad on weekends," Maureen protested. She tried to explain. "That's the only time we see each other since the separation. Besides, it's sort of lonely around my house on weekends. My mom's busy showing houses then. It's her busiest time. And I'd be sitting by myself in that big house waiting for the phone to ring. Yuck! And even if it did ring, it would be someone wanting an appointment with my mom."

"You're exaggerating," Debbie scoffed.

"Anyway, most of the boys around here are so dumb," Maureen continued. "All they're interested in is spectator sports. Larry Bird this! Red Sox that! Play-offs! Batting averages! I just can't bring myself to care who wins those games, and I'm not going to pretend I do."

Debbie said nothing, but she looked surprised at Maureen's outburst.

The other spectators on Heartbreak Hill were starting to drift away. The front runners were probably nearing the finish line at the Prudential Center amid a crush of TV film crews, motorcycle cops, and cheering fans.

Beacon Street was still clogged with slower runners now—the local teachers, housewives, businessmen, and students for whom this was a once-a-year ritual rather than a way of life. A slow, plodding pack of tired, sweaty bodies, agonizing over every step.

Still absorbed in the race, Maureen was clapping hard for the stragglers. "Come on, you can make it! You're almost there!" she called out to number four hundred fifty-three, who was staring straight ahead, a faraway look in her eyes as she resolutely placed one foot in front of the other. Her soaking-wet ponytail bounced limply against her back as she ran.

To Maureen, the race was still exciting. She loved calling out to the runners, encouraging them, seeing their pace pick up a bit in response to the support of the crowd. She had been to Fenway Park once, to see the Red Sox play, but her seat had been so far away from the action, she couldn't even see the ball—not like here, where you could practically reach out and touch the runners and see the expressions on their faces as they pushed themselves harder and harder.

Maureen admired them all, even those who straggled in late in the day after the TV cameras were long gone, when the streets were no longer barricaded, and only the large mounds of trash piled near the curb indicated that it had been marathon day. Twenty-six-plus miles! That was an accomplishment no matter how long it took.

But Debbie was getting bored. "Come on, let's

go home. I'm exhausted just watching. We can go to my house and have a Coke and see the rest of the race on TV. They're probably interviewing the winners right now."

Maureen continued cheering enthusiastically.

"Look, Mo, the rest'll just have to make it without our help. I'm too thirsty to stay another minute!" Debbie said firmly, pulling her friend away from the curb before Maureen could notice anyone else who might need encouragement.

As the two girls walked down the tree-lined street toward Debbie's house, Maureen tried to explain. "You don't understand what a great thing it is to run a marathon."

"It's true. I don't," Debbie replied. "Every time I have to run to catch the trolley into Boston I get so out of breath I can't talk for fifteen minutes."

Maureen couldn't help laughing. "If you started running every day, you'd be in a lot better shape, Debbie. I don't understand how someone barely sixteen years old can be so weak."

"I don't, either. Maybe I'm built for comfort, not for speed, as the song goes." They both laughed.

Maureen knew that she, however, was definitely built for speed. Her mother used to complain that Maureen had never learned to walk. It was a family joke that she had gone straight from crawling to running.

As a kid she had spent many happy hours zipping around her neighborhood imagining she was a cowgirl racing across the plains while her more lethargic friends relaxed with *The Brady Bunch.*

They continued walking down the street, immersed in their own thoughts. The occasional runner still plodded by, but the girls paid no attention. As they turned into Debbie's street, Maureen finally broke the silence.

"Did you know the first marathons were run barefoot? No fancy running shoes!"

"Really?" Debbie looked impressed.

"Yeah, my dad told me that. He tells me lots of interesting stuff. You know, about history."

"I think that's kind of neat. My dad talks mostly about interest rates, which is a little hard to relate to."

Debbie opened her front door and immediately kicked off her shoes, collapsing onto the sofa with a groan. "I think I'm starting to identify with those runners. My feet hurt just from walking back from Heartbreak Hill. That was a little farther than I'd expected."

"How about that Coke?" Maureen reminded her as she turned on the TV and flipped through the channels looking for the marathon.

"Oh, sure. I'll get some."

"Hey, Debbie," Maureen called after her. "What's Jake's last name?"

"Harmon. H-A-R-M-O-N. Why?"

Maureen smiled to herself, remembering his tall, lanky body and warm, brown eyes.

"Let's look him up in the phone book. I want to find out where he lives."

Two

On Wednesday it turned cool—perfect running weather. Maureen hurried home from school eager to begin her daily workout. Maybe once she started running her head would clear. She hadn't been able to concentrate on anything since the marathon two days before.

Maureen went up to her room and studied herself in the mirror. Not bad. Her face was flushed and her cheeks rosy. Her blond hair was pulled back off her face with a colorful hair ribbon. When she was a kid, she'd worn it short and curly, like Shirley Temple. Now it reached down her back in long waves. Her hair was definitely her best feature, Maureen decided. And she was pretty, although certainly not "gorgeous," as her parents always said. In movies, girls with long legs and hair like hers dated team captains—but so far, these attributes hadn't gotten *her* anywhere.

Thank goodness she wasn't a pale, freckly

blonde. She could get a nice tan in the summer. Sometimes her arms and legs would get really dark, a chestnut color, and when she ran hard she almost felt like a horse—galloping free, brown legs pounding, and golden mane blowing in the wind. It was a neat feeling.

She quickly changed into her running clothes and went down to the living room to begin to stretch, grasping the door jamb firmly with both hands and sliding one leg out behind her. She bounced slowly, pushing her outstretched heel down to the floor and gently stretching out her Achilles tendon.

Maureen couldn't stop thinking about the boy she'd seen at the race on Monday. "Jake Harmon," she said out loud, practicing the sound. Even though she knew where he lived and his phone number now, she had no intention of calling him up. She would never be able to do that. Asking for dates was one thing Maureen was happy to leave to the boys. *And look what good that's done you,* she thought, reflecting on her dateless career. With a sigh, she switched legs and continued to stretch.

She knew from having looked up his address that Jake lived on one of those curving roads behind the reservoir. It was a nice area—big houses with well-kept lawns backing up to the peanut-shaped pond. A path circled the water, bounded by weeping willows and flowering trees that shaded strollers on sunny days.

She stood up and dropped over, reaching her hands to the floor. In spite of her long legs, she easily placed her palms flat and pressed her head to her knees, stretching out her hamstrings. Heavy honey-colored curls tumbled down, covering her feet, then falling in her face as she stood up.

She remembered Jake's hair. She liked how it curled around his ears, dark brown with a hint of red in the sun.

Sitting down, she tucked her toes under the sofa, locked her fingers behind her head, and started her sit-ups. She wondered if Jake liked to run. Maybe he just liked to photograph runners. And, then again, maybe he didn't care about runners at all but just needed to get some photos for the paper.

"Twenty-four . . . twenty-five . . . twenty-six . . ." she whispered to herself. She didn't feel any strain at all, yet.

He had been wearing running shoes, but everyone did now. It was like a uniform—nothing to do with running. She looked at her own well-worn New Balance shoes. Almost time for a new pair. ". . . Forty . . . seven . . . forty . . . eight . . . forty . . . nine . . . fifty!" Now she could feel it. A good burn. It told her she was working hard.

13

On her way out, Maureen poked her head into her mother's office on the first floor of their house. " 'Bye, Mom. Be back in an hour." Mrs. Meyer, with the phone tucked onto her shoulder and pencil in hand, smiled and nodded as Maureen took off on her afternoon run.

The trouble with Riverton was the hills. The streets curved gently up, down, and around, creating a tree-lined labyrinth. Once, totally confused by the maze of turns, Maureen had gotten lost and took an extra hour to find her way home. For the next few weeks, she had run with a miniature map tucked into the pocket of her shorts just in case. Also, there was hardly a flat street in the whole town. They climbed or fell, varying only in the steepness of the angle. Even the slightest grade could cause pain if you weren't used to it. But then she always pushed herself a little. If it didn't hurt some, she didn't feel as though she'd done enough.

She was halfway up a big one now. Summit Hill. She could see all of Boston from the top. The ache in her calves broke her train of thought, forcing her to concentrate on her running. Keep going. Put one foot in front of the other. Don't slow down. Steady. Pace it. She talked herself up to the top.

Going down didn't require so much concentration, so her mind drifted to Jake. Suddenly her feet felt lighter. Jake. She had to find a way to meet him again, but it would be hard at school. They didn't share any classes, not even lunch. Not much chance of running into him. She wasn't one for starting conversations in the hall, anyway. Or at all, as a matter of fact. Maybe she could think of a reason to hang around the yearbook office. Then she could ask to see the marathon photos. Of course they'd be terrific, and she would admire them and ask him to tell her how to take good pictures.

She wondered if Jake would be hard to talk to. Everyone always told her to talk to a boy about something that interested the boy. But that wasn't as easy as it sounded. What if you didn't know what he was interested in, or if you did, what if you didn't know anything about that subject? Maureen wondered, feeling frustrated. She liked to read Dear Beth and Dear Abby, and the columnists' advice always seemed great for other people's problems. But when she tried to apply it to her own life, the solution was never as easy as it sounded. Things were always more complicated. For instance, she would have to learn something about photography before discussing it with Jake, or she'd sound like a real dope.

As she ran, Maureen glanced around. Spring was the best season for running—if it wasn't raining, of course. The air smelled fresh and good, and she could look around while she ran, enjoying the spring flowers, especially the trees. Riverton had so many flowering trees—cherry, apple, dogwood, even magnolia. It wasn't quite so colorful as her old neighborhood near Philadelphia where almost every yard had azalea bushes in multiple shades of purple and pink. But Riverton—and Boston—were nice.

Life had been simpler in Philadelphia. Her father had been a philosophy professor at a small college. His department had been eliminated because of low enrollment and budget problems, and he felt he had been lucky to get another teaching job in Boston. *Very* lucky, he kept reminding her.

She had cried when she found out she wouldn't be going to Darby High with her friends. She had bitterly resented her parents then and had wondered how they could have done that to her—just pack up and move—making her leave all her friends behind. Logically, she knew they couldn't help it, but the move had been hard for her to adjust to.

Maybe her dad was lucky, but Maureen felt as if moving to Riverton was when her luck had begun to run out. They had only been there two months, hardly enough time to learn her way around the city, when everything changed: her father moved out. Her wonderful, handsome, funny, caring father was gone.

Weekends were the worst. It was then that

Maureen felt her loneliness most. The house was so quiet, she felt like screaming. Her mom had started working for a real estate broker and was always out showing houses. Just when Maureen needed to talk, she was on her own.

She hadn't even had a good friend to talk things over with. At least she had Debbie now, but it still made her mad to think about those first few months. She still didn't understand why her parents had gotten a separation. She knew that a lot of the kids in her school lived with only one parent, but that didn't make it any easier for her.

She had been really naive, too. She refused to believe it when her mother told her they were splitting up. Maureen had felt certain that her dad would be back. There hadn't been any fights, not even a serious argument—in front of her, at least. She had always thought they were happy. But, as they both tried to explain to her in a long and awful discussion one night, they weren't. She was in high school now, they reminded her. Their separation had nothing to do with her. They both still loved her, and they knew she'd be able to handle it. Well, she had "handled" it. But she didn't like it.

Maureen swore out loud. As she started to feel angry thinking about the separation, her stride lengthened, her feet pounded the pavement, her heart raced to keep up with her legs.

All the going back and forth between them and their houses, she thought. It was a big pain. She felt split down the middle. She always carried some of her things around with her in a huge canvas tote bag. And her schoolbooks alone filled one backpack. The rest of her possessions she had divided up and left in one of her two bedrooms. No matter how organized she was, though, or how far ahead she planned, she always seemed to need something that had been left at the other house.

Trying to live two lives was very frustrating. She could see how some kids just gave up after a while—like her friend Danny, back in Philadelphia. When his parents first got divorced, he spent schooldays with his mother and weekends with his father. Then that changed so that he was spending most of the school year with his mother and vacations with his father. Then finally his father moved to California, and they talked a lot on the telephone. Of course, that would never happen to her, Maureen knew, because her dad was special. But she felt her stomach tighten with fear, anyway. She *had* to keep seeing her dad regularly. She couldn't bear it if he were ever to move far away.

Taking a deep breath, she sprinted ahead. Running made her feel better. As she ran, her mind was free to sort things out. Her legs carried her down the sidewalk, across streets, into

18

familiar neighborhoods, or off in new directions almost of their own accord. Sometimes she ran the exact same route, for weeks. It was comforting to see familiar faces, strangers still, but at least familiar, and to know that some things—places, anyway—didn't change. It made her feel secure. The dogs got used to seeing her, and the kids waved hello.

Other times she would take off in new directions, see parts of the city she had never seen before. She didn't always know where her run would lead, but she was calling the shots.

Maureen looked up, at last noticing her surroundings. The houses were starting to get bigger and be spaced farther apart. The yards were nicely landscaped, the hedges trimmed. Even the cars in the driveways were shinier. She was approaching the reservoir. With Jake so much on her mind, she had found her way to his neighborhood. Not a total surprise, she had to admit. In the back of her mind, she had known where her legs were leading her. She crossed the street and ran up the path past the old pumping station to the dirt track and joined the runners already making the rounds.

A large German shepherd's barking and snapping rudely broke into her thoughts. *Why can't people keep their monsters on leashes?* she wondered.

"Max, heel! Heel!"

Maureen turned her head, almost tripping over her feet. She felt as if someone had hit her in the stomach and knocked all the air out of her when she saw who was rushing up to snap a leash on Max's collar. Because she didn't know what to do, she continued running, slowing down a little so that Jake and Max fell into step beside her. It was her Big Chance. But Maureen felt as if she'd been struck dumb. Her feet were still going, but it was as though her brain cells had become glued together. Nothing was moving up there. She couldn't think of a thing to say! Yet here he was—the very person she'd been daydreaming about!

"You're Debbie's friend, aren't you? I remember you from the marathon. I'm Jake Harmon. Do you live around here?"

Tongue-tied, Maureen shook her head.

"I usually come over here to give Maximillian a run. He's really well trained, but sometimes he does chase runners. I keep him on the leash if he gets obnoxious. Do you run here a lot?" Jake asked.

"Mmm, sometimes," Maureen mumbled.

She was jogging slowly now, but Jake and Max were straining to keep pace with a fast walk. Max seemed able to run and bark at the same time, but Jake was beginning to have trouble keeping up the conversation.

"Hey, could you either slow down or say something so I can catch my breath? I'm not used to this sort of thing."

Abruptly, Jake turned off the path and flopped down on one of the benches that ringed the pond. Max obediently sat by his side while Maureen had no choice but to stop, too. She continued running in place on the path in front of them, though.

"What's your name, anyway?"

"Maureen Meyer."

"How about taking a break, Maureen," Jake offered. "Sit down with us and watch the ducks." A small boy nearby was tossing bread crumbs into the water, and about fifty ducks were quacking hungrily as if they hadn't eaten in weeks.

Maureen noticed that there were glints of red and gold in his thick brown hair. She loved the way it was blown back from his face by the wind. Jake's eyes were warm and inviting, and for a moment she wavered and then felt herself start toward the bench.

But no! What was she doing? Here she was, all hot and sweaty, dressed in her worst-looking sweatshirt and shorts. Her hair was dirty, she probably looked awful, she didn't even know him—what would they talk about? The ducks?

Flustered and embarrassed, Maureen backed

up onto the jogging path. She was going to blow it, she knew. But she just couldn't help it; she didn't have the nerve to sit down with him. Only one thing was on her mind then—escape.

"Sorry, I—I can't stop jogging in the middle of a run. I'm—I'm in training. Got to go."

Turning abruptly, Maureen ran away. He had caught her off guard. It wasn't fair! Why did people always have to show up before she was ready?

Why couldn't she talk to boys the way she did to girls? What was wrong with her? Maureen clenched her fists as she ran. She tried to be a good listener, which was what her mother always advised, but that obviously wasn't enough. How did other girls, like Debbie, do it? Sometimes Maureen felt as if there were some gigantic secret that she hadn't been let in on yet, some club—the girls-who-can-talk-to-boys club—to which she still needed membership before anything could happen.

This is ridiculous, Maureen thought. *I'm an intelligent person. I know what's going on in the world.* And yet she hadn't come across a single boy who wanted to talk about current events. She tried to remember whether the Red Sox were winning or losing, but it never seemed to work for her. Obviously this was an area where she needed help—before it was too late.

As she ran home, she kept thinking of the expression of surprise on Jake's face as she had suddenly turned and run off. He probably wasn't used to girls literally running away from him. When she got home, Maureen ran through the house and up to the bathroom. A hot shower would relax her and maybe even give her some ideas for her next meeting with Jake. "Next time I'll be ready for it," she muttered as the scalding water beat down on her head.

"Well, if you weren't able to think of a word to say, you could always have 'accidentally' tripped and fallen down just in front of him," Debbie offered after hearing Maureen's version of how she had blown her big chance with Jake. "Then he would have rushed to your side, taken you in his arms, and . . . well, neither of you would have needed any words after that!"

But when she saw the stricken look on her friend's face, Debbie's smile faded. "Oh, Mo, don't worry—look on the bright side of things. He remembered you! He *tried* to get to know you. And, at least, you did manage to tell him your name. So, actually, you've made a lot of progress."

"Yeah, I guess he must have been a little interested in me," Maureen admitted, hoping against hope that Debbie was right.

"Now all you have to do is run over to the

reservoir at around the same time. The odds are, you're bound to meet him again. He just lives around the corner. It'll be easier to talk to him there than here at school, anyway, because too many other kids are always around here."

"But I'm so embarrassed. He probably thinks I'm a snob, or worse. You don't know how dumb I acted," Maureen protested, starting to feel desperate again. "I just stood there, running in place with a silly grin on my face, not saying a single word. Anyway, I can't go back right away."

"How come?"

"Today's Friday, and I'm going up to my dad's right after school."

"Well, don't worry about it," Debbie said soothingly. "By Monday Jake will have forgotten everything but those beautiful blond curls of yours. He probably thinks you're mysterious. It never hurts to play hard to get, you know."

If playing hard to get really fascinates them, Maureen thought skeptically, *then Jake ought to be totally bedazzled.*

But later that afternoon, as Maureen waited for the trolley that would take her to Cambridge, she thought more seriously about Debbie's advice. She had never noticed her friend playing hard to get, and yet Debbie had more invitations than she knew what to do with. Even during her first year and a half of high school, when her teeth had been studded with metal

24

bands, Debbie had constantly been asked out. The braces had never been a bother because her good sense of humor always enabled her to laugh off things like that. And now Debbie's reward was a set of nicely aligned teeth and what everyone agreed was a truly beautiful smile.

Debbie really knew what she was talking about when it came to dating, Maureen decided. There was no need to write for advice with such a local "expert" around. She made a mental note to discuss her strategy with Debbie as soon as she got back on Monday.

Three

The worst part of visiting her dad was carrying her heavy tote bag all the way from the station at Harvard Square up Brattle Street to his apartment. The ride itself wasn't bad. It took about ten minutes to get to Kenmore Square from her house. At Kenmore Square the trolley cars went underground, and it took about twenty more minutes on the subway to Harvard Square, and then she had the walk.

Halfway there that afternoon, Maureen set her bag down with a groan and wiggled her cramped shoulder around to loosen the muscles. A moment later, she picked it up again and trudged on. She had only brought a few things—her running shoes, warm-up suit, and some odds and ends, plus a weekend's worth of homework. But all together it amounted to a heavy load; and by the time she reached her dad's door, she had changed hands five or six times, and her fingers were numb. She would have to learn to travel light.

"Dad, it's me," she called out, unlocking the front door and stepping inside.

"Hi, honey. Be with you in a minute. Come in and fix yourself a snack."

Putting down her bag, Maureen glanced around and suddenly felt very happy that she'd come. Immediately she headed for her father's kitchen. Every square inch of wall space was filled with shelves and cupboards, and a lot of those shelves contained snacks: peanuts, chips, pretzels, popcorn, health food, junk food, all mixed together. A big bowl of fruit sat on a tiny table, which was pushed up against a window overlooking a fenced-in courtyard. There were even cookies and, worst of all, a package of Twinkies. Norm Meyer was a nibbler. He often stayed up late working in his study and never wanted to run the risk of being hungry at three in the morning and finding nothing to munch on.

Maureen, trying to decide between potato chips and ice cream, helped herself to both. Eating was a lot of fun at her dad's house. They both loved food and ate all kinds of things—whenever they felt like it, too. Meals didn't have to be at a certain time, and desserts could be as big as she wanted. She wondered if her father knew what calories were. He certainly didn't give them much thought if he did. When you ran four or five miles a day as he did, you could eat just about anything you wanted to.

That started her thinking about her mother's kitchen. It was a cheerful, almost beautiful room. Copper pots hung on a reddish brick wall. Warm light filtering through the leaves of hanging plants flooded the room. The red tile floor and the oak cabinets and table gave it a warm, earthy feeling. There were usually fresh flowers on the table in a stoneware vase that her mother had made in a pottery class once. It was a comfortable room, a nice place to come home to.

As a kitchen, however, it was almost nonfunctional. The copper pots on the wall were for decoration only. Her mother never cooked. Salads were their mainstay—tossed salad, fruit salad, tuna salad, chicken salad, bean salad, egg salad . . . Their refrigerator got a lot more use than the spotlessly clean stove, which stood in the corner. Not only did Mrs. Meyer seem to subsist on salads alone, but she also allowed no junk food in the house. She was watching her weight and didn't want to be tempted. Sugar had been banned without exception. No cookies, cakes, or candy ever passed through the door. Fortunately, a special exception was made for holidays. For the most part, though, Maureen had to save her urge to indulge herself for the weekends.

She opened the refrigerator and found a *real* Coke. *Might as well go all the way,* she thought, washing down the chips with the Coke. *I can always run it off later.*

"Pour one for me, too, honey," Mr. Meyer called in from his study. Maureen heard a book snap shut, and soon her father joined her at the kitchen table.

"I saw you on TV last week," he said.

"TV? I wasn't on TV!"

"Yes, you were. On Heartbreak Hill. The camera panned the crowd, and there you were, cheering your heart out and looking fantastic."

Maureen was amazed. How neat that she'd been on TV! Had anyone else seen her? If so, why had no one said anything? *Probably because, still, hardly anyone knows who I am,* she realized glumly. Smiling quickly, she said, "Watching the race was fun. Debbie and I went."

"I didn't know I had such a beautiful daughter. Must have been your mother's side of the family."

"Oh, come on, Dad," Maureen protested. People often said she was pretty, but somehow she never was able to believe them. Her father was the worst offender. He'd probably think she was gorgeous even if she had two noses!

"How come you're not a cheerleader? All those dance lessons you had could be put to some use. Didn't you ever try out for the squad?"

"Uh-uh."

"But you'd make a terrific cheerleader. When I saw you out there clapping away, I wanted to grab my shoes and get out there and climb that hill!"

"Daddy," she groaned, "why would I want to be a cheerleader? If I did *anything*, I'd want to compete, not just clap for someone else!"

Mr. Meyer nodded. "I see what you mean. But everyone can't be a star, you know. Someone's got to stay behind the scenes and provide support."

"Maybe 'someone.' But why me?"

"I agree. It shouldn't be you. You are definitely star material."

Maureen looked at her father. His tone was serious. "Really, Dad?"

"Sure. I can recognize talent when I see it. If you genuinely want to do something, why don't you enter a race? Maybe not the marathon, something a little shorter."

"I'm not sure I want to race. I just like running."

"Well, think it over. I bet you'd do well. Come on, let's get changed and stretch our legs a little."

Fifteen minutes later Maureen and her dad were heading down the driveway and into the street toward Fresh Pond. As they ran, they passed a variety of people—college kids in their school T-shirts, graduate students who looked more serious, young mothers with their babies in strollers, and many other joggers.

Maureen was always amused by the number of pretty girls who ran in makeup and jewelry, outfitted in the latest running gear from Bloomingdale's, trying to remain as beautiful and unwilted as possible while they ran. Fat, skinny, young, and old, all sorts of people were heading toward the tree-lined pond.

"Dad, remember when I first started running seriously? Even though I was in good shape, it still took me ten minutes to do the mile around the reservoir, and I couldn't even make it around Fresh Pond without stopping to catch my breath."

"Sure do. Now we do this run all the time, and I don't have to slow down for you anymore. I think if you really pushed yourself I'd have trouble keeping up with you now," her father said, proud of her rapid progress.

"Those first few months after we moved from Philadelphia were awful," Maureen said, thinking back. "I couldn't find anyone my own age in Riverton. Everyone was either working or down at the Cape for the summer. I used to sit out in the yard, reading, hoping to discover some kids walking by. But no one ever did—a few old ladies with dogs, that was all. Hardly anyone under fifty went by until the end of August."

"Weren't there any kids over at the pool?"

"I tried that. I remember when I went for a long walk and found the high school. It was huge, so I knew there must be a lot of teenagers around somewhere, but the pool was filled with day campers, and the gym had been taken over by the under-ten set. I tried to get to know some of their counselors, but they were too busy to socialize."

"I know you really missed your old friends. They were a nice bunch of kids, and you'd known them all for such a long time," her father commented, his voice sympathetic.

"Yeah, I'd never been on my own like that before. I'd always had friends and lots of things to do."

"I guess we were both a little lonely then. Being on my own was new for me, too," Mr. Meyer admitted.

They started around at a pretty fast pace, nodding at familiar faces and staring past people who weren't regulars. Maureen realized she felt less lonely as a runner, a part of the dedicated crowd of people who didn't really know one another but shared the same daily ritual.

"Jogging was just right for us," Maureen said. "At least it was something we could do alone if we had to. Well, not exactly *alone*! We always have a lot of company," she continued. "No matter what time of day or night or what kind of weather, there'll be other people running—even when the temperature is over ninety-five and people are warned to stay indoors."

"I'm a dedicated runner, but not *that* dedicated. I also draw the line at blizzards."

"And hurricanes."

"And tornadoes."

"How about earthquakes?"

"You bet. I would never run during an earthquake."

"Me, neither," Maureen added, giggling. "But sometimes I think about how nice it would be if we could have the path to ourselves for once. It's easy to get tired of the crowds. On a nice day like today, you practically have to signal when you want to turn!"

Her father chuckled as they rounded the far end of the pond, and they ran on talking and reminiscing. Soon Maureen began to feel exhilarated. Worries seemed to fade away when you were running hard. After a while, she stopped thinking about Jake, her dad, everything. She only heard the rhythmical thump of running shoes on the dirt path and her own slow, regular breathing. The air smelled fresh and good.

"Do you really think I should enter a race, Dad?"

"Sure I do. You'd have to train a little more seriously for a while, but I know you could do it. And I'd be really proud of you."

They ran in silence again as Maureen tried to

imagine herself in the marathon, taking Heart-break Hill in perfect form—inching ahead of the others, then flying to the front. The street before her was clear, the crowds standing along the sides cheering wildly and clapping. People held out paper cups of water for her to grab and drink as she ran. She glanced back—she was still in the lead!

Her legs ached, her lungs felt as if they were going to burst, but Maureen knew she was al-most at the finish line, about to break a world's record! Looking over to the side, she saw that the route was lined with all the kids from Coo-lidge High, cheering and waving. At the finish line was Jake, camera poised as she broke through the tape to set a new women's record. Then he was running toward her, smiling, laughing—sweeping her into his arms.

The honk of a car's horn in the distance sud-denly brought Maureen back to reality, and she sighed. As she and her father left the secluded path that ringed the sanctuary, they plunged into the heavy traffic on the narrow, twisting streets of Cambridge. As the stoplight changed to red, the two paused at the curb, jogging in place as the cars went by, bumper to bumper. Another pair of joggers came up from behind and impatiently darted into the street against the light, weaving through the stream of cars to the sound of blasting horns and squealing brakes.

"People like those two give runners a bad name," Mr. Meyer said. "It's hard enough to drive around here without having people running in front of you all the time. I'd hate to be one of your driver-training teachers at school. That must be a nerve-racking job."

"Yeah, two of them quit last year. Couldn't take the pressure. I think they have to pass calmness tests before they're allowed to take kids on the road."

Her legs ached now, but they kept up the pace till they reached their usual landmark, an incredible tree trunk, stripped of bark and branches, which had been carved by some unknown sculptor into the shape of a gigantic hand reaching toward the sky. From there, they always walked the last few blocks to cool down. Sweat poured down their faces, wet shirts clung to their backs, despite the fact that the day was not a warm one.

It was funny, but she felt closer to her dad then than she had before, Maureen realized. Even though they didn't live together as a family anymore, they got together regularly and didn't take each other for granted. He always wanted to know all about what she was doing in school and how she felt about everything. They talked about all kinds of things, especially while they ran, which made Maureen feel really grown-up. She wondered if she should tell him about Jake. Of course, there really wasn't anything to tell, but . . .

Maureen stole a glance at her father and then began, shyly, "Dad . . . you know, at the marathon? I met somebody." She paused.

"Oh, tell me about him."

"His name is Jake. He's a friend of Debbie's, sort of, and he's a photographer."

"What kind of stuff does he do?"

"Oh, he takes pictures for the yearbook, and he gets photos published in the *Gazette* and a few other places. At least that's what Debbie said."

"I supposed he's already reserved your weekends for the next six months."

All at once, Maureen felt silly. "Not exactly, Dad. He hasn't asked me out yet. In fact, I've never really even talked to him."

"Well, I guess things haven't gotten too serious yet. I don't have to worry about his knocking on my door someday to ask for your hand."

"Dad, don't tease," Maureen blurted out, frustrated. Her dad was a guy, maybe he could tell her what to do. "I want him to like me, but when I meet him, I panic. My mind goes totally blank, and I can't think of a thing to say. That's always been my problem around boys, but with

Jake it really upsets me, because I'd like to get to know him."

"Maybe you're just trying too hard. I know this sounds corny, but just be yourself. You're a very likable person. You don't have to say or do anything brilliant to impress him."

"But, Dad, I'm not talking about brilliant, I'm talking about words of more than one syllable. I'm not kidding," Maureen said desperately. "I ran into him at the reservoir the other day, and I could barely say my name. I'm sure he thinks I'm a number-one nerd."

"I doubt it. Maybe he isn't as hard on you as you think he is. Give him a chance. Anyway, next time let him do the talking. If you really have things in common, you'll discover them."

"If there is a next time . . . He probably won't even bother talking to me again," Maureen said, refusing to be encouraged.

"Of course he will. If he gives up that easily, then he's the nerd. When you see him, just remember he's probably trying just as hard to impress you!"

That was an interesting idea, Maureen thought. Was it possible that Jake was as nervous around her as she was around him? She closed her eyes, trying to imagine handsome Jake tongue-tied and uneasy. Impossible!

"OK, Dad. Thanks," she said. But deep inside, Maureen knew better. Jake was obviously one boy who knew where he was going and what he wanted. The question was, could she ever make him believe that *she* was what he wanted?

Four

"Maureen! Maureen! I've finally found you! You weren't at lunch. I've been trying to get hold of you all day."

Maureen was sitting on the cement steps of the old gym trying to remember her math assignment. Was it the even-numbered problems on the odd pages or the odd ones on the even pages that she was supposed to do?

As she heard Debbie's high-heeled sandals tapping rapidly toward her on the sidewalk, she glanced up. Why anyone would try to run even a few feet in those things was a mystery to Maureen. But they did make Debbie look very fashionable. Together with her oversized white shirt with black-and-red Japanese calligraphy and her large red earrings, the shoes made her look twenty-five instead of fifteen.

Debbie managed to run up the stairs without tripping over the piles of books and jackets strewn around and sat down beside Maureen.

"You sure have been making yourself scarce today."

Maureen rolled her eyes and nodded. "I had to write twenty vocabulary sentences for English. I didn't get a chance to do them this weekend, so I thought I'd better skip lunch. Mr. Devon got really mad last week when I turned in my homework after school."

"I've been dying to tell you something," Debbie blurted out, ignoring her explanation. "My mom said I could have a party next Saturday!"

"Oh, Debbie!" Maureen cried, sitting up straight with excitement. This would be a great chance for her to make some more friends and meet guys. Then, disappointment struck her.

"Don't worry. It won't be a couples party. I'll ask a lot of different people. I'll even ask more boys than girls."

"Make it at least two to one—maybe even three to one," Maureen said ruefully.

"I don't think I know that many cute boys," Debbie said, laughing. "We'd be scraping the bottom of the barrel, so to speak. Wouldn't two or three extras be enough? Then if a few of them started talking about sports, there'd still be enough guys to dance with."

"I guess so. What kind of party is it going to be?"

"I don't know. What do you think?"

"Mmmmm. It's not your birthday. Nobody's

moving away. There's no holiday coming up, except Mother's Day. How about a swimming party? We could all meet at the pool, then go over to your house afterward."

"No, I'd hate to go to a party all wet. My hair would be a mess."

"How about a pizza party? A make-your-own pizza party! You can buy the dough. Then you just roll it out, and all the kids can put on the stuff they like—mushrooms, pepperoni, whatever—and you bake them."

"That's a great idea!" Debbie agreed, looking pleased. She cocked her head and asked, "You sure they come out OK? I've only made frozen ones."

"Sure, they're terrific. My mom makes them when she feels like cooking. We make whole wheat, but I think the regular pizza dough works better. It comes out crispier."

"Gee, I didn't know you knew so much about cooking, Mo."

"Well, I don't, actually. Making pizza isn't really cooking. It's more like . . . uh . . . melting. You just stick everything on, put it in the oven, and it melts. Nothing to it."

"OK. I'm convinced. But you have to come over and help me get everything ready."

"No problem. I'm very good at chopping. I'm always slicing up vegetables for one thing or another."

"I didn't know you had all these hidden abilities! Good looks and talent, too! Wow! Now for the invitations. Let's make a list."

"How many can you have?"

"Twenty, max, because we're going to have to stay downstairs in the family room. I was thinking nine girls and eleven boys."

"How about twelve. Your parents will never notice one extra boy. And probably at least one won't show up, anyway."

"Yeah, you're right. It wouldn't hurt to ask twelve."

As they walked home from school that afternoon, the girls decided on the final guest list. They picked the boys first, then went on to discuss which girls to include.

"How about Karen Rider?" Maureen asked. "She's an old friend of yours, isn't she?"

"She *was* an old friend. She's been acting so snobby lately. It would serve her right if we left her out."

"You know, Debbie, we'll have to invite Karen if we want to get Brian to come. I've seen them together at least three times this week."

"You're right. OK. I'll give her one more chance. We've got to have Brian, or Kevin and Alex might not come. Those three are inseparable."

Maureen shook her head. "I never realized how complicated having a simple pizza party could get."

They had so much more to talk about that they stood on the corner in front of Debbie's house for ten more minutes. They added and crossed out names until they had the perfect combination of guests. Finally sitting down on the steps in front of her house, they planned the refreshments. When all the details were settled, Maureen and Debbie split up, each with a list of things to do and people to call.

As soon as Maureen got home, she realized she had to do one thing immediately—decide what to wear! Running upstairs, she quickly tore through her closet. Nothing looked right. She had a lot of clothes, but not many dresses, and they had decided to wear dresses to the party. The boys wouldn't dress up, but it would be more fun, Debbie had decided, if the girls looked nice.

Maureen groaned out loud as she pawed through her hangers for the second time. Everything seemed either too plain or too fancy.

She ran downstairs and found her mother making dinner in the kitchen. "Mom, Debbie's giving a party, and I'm helping plan it, and I need a new dress," she announced in one breath. "And, also, can you help us make your tomato-sauce recipe? It's going to be a pizza party. We're serving homemade pizzas with the works."

"Well, let's see, honey. Of course I'll help with the tomato sauce, and I guess you can have a new dress, too. Remember our bargain, though. You pay half, with your own money, for nonessentials."

"OK, Mom, but this is an essential. My future social life depends on this party, and I won't feel comfortable unless I'm wearing the right dress."

Mrs. Meyer laughed. "I know how you feel. That is pretty important, but I can still only afford half."

Maureen paused, making a few quick mental calculations. "OK. I still have some birthday money left from Grandma Meyer."

"How about going shopping on Thursday before dinner? I won't schedule any late-afternoon appointments, and we'll run over to the mall and take a quick look. Then you'll still have the weekend to try somewhere else if we don't have any luck."

"Great! Thanks, Mom."

"Now, how about giving me a hand with these vegetables?" Mrs. Meyer added slyly. "While I make the dressing—*your* favorite."

Maureen was so excited and happy during dinner that she didn't think about the phone calls she had to make until afterward. The girls would be no problem, but when she realized she had to call boys, too, her stomach did a flip-flop. She had to call that night because Debbie wanted to know who could come as soon as possible.

Dragging her heels, Maureen took the upstairs hall phone with the long cord into her room and shut the door. She started down the list. Karen Rider . . . nobody home. Next, Jennifer Piatelli . . . the line was busy. Maybe her mom could give her some pointers; she was always on the phone for business, and she sounded marvelous—confident and self-assured. She began to wish she had paid more attention to her mom's technique: eventually someone would answer, and she'd have to say something.

Maureen's first conversation was with someone's ten-year-old brother; her next was with an answering machine. Now that she had exhausted the names of the girls on her list, it was time to start on the guys. Mike Eldridge was the first name she had written down. This one might not be too hard, she thought, trying to fool herself into thinking it was no big deal. After all, she saw him every day in English class. He'd be good to practice on.

"Hi, Mike? This is Maureen. Uh, how's your report coming along?"

"Oh, hi, Maureen. Actually, I haven't started writing it yet. I'm still trying to find some books in the library. The one I need most has been checked out for two weeks. I'm going to be in big trouble if I don't get that book soon."

"I'm not too far along, either. I got the books, though, so at least that's one problem I don't have. Umm, Mike, the reason I called is Debbie asked me to help organize this party she's having next Saturday. It's a pizza party with dancing down in her rec room."

"Sounds like fun."

"Do you think you can come?"

"Uh, yeah. I think so. When does it start?"

"Oh, be there around seven."

"OK. Thanks for the invitation."

"Glad you can come. 'Bye."

Maureen hung up and breathed a sigh of relief. All right, she had a yes from a nice guy, and she'd carried on a decent conversation without saying anything horribly dumb! The next few calls also went smoothly. As she checked off the names on her list, she got closer to the one she still dreaded: Jake Harmon. Debbie had insisted that Maureen make that call, even though she had protested that there were a hundred reasons why she couldn't.

Maureen stared at the phone. She hummed to herself as she dialed the number, listening to the sound of the beeps a few times but always hanging up before the first ring. She sharpened her pencil. She started doodling on the message pad and filled an entire page with geometric shapes. She went back down to the kitchen and poured herself a Tab. This was it. She had to do it, she thought, as she walked back upstairs sipping the Tab.

Just as she was reaching for the receiver, the phone rang. "Arghh!" she cried, so startled she almost dropped her drink. Picking it up, Maureen heard a familiar voice.

"Hi, Mo. How's it going?" asked Debbie.

"Well, I talked to three kids, a mother, a brother, and an answering machine, but it wasn't too hard," Maureen replied, ignoring her pounding heart.

"Is everyone you talked to coming?"

"So far. But, Debbie, you know you could really do me a gigantic favor if you called Jake. I just don't know him well enough to ask him to a party. And it's your party, anyway. He might think I'm asking him as my date. Couldn't you please, please call him? I'll do your math homework for a week if you do it."

"Maureen!"

"Two weeks?"

"No, Maureen. You've got to do it. Believe me, I know best. Just say you're helping me call the guests. You have to show him you're interested in him."

"But I'll sound dumb. He'll never come. You would do it so much better. I'm terrible at invitations."

"Practice makes perfect, Mo. Now, no more excuses," Debbie said, her voice firm. "I'm going to call back in an hour, and you'd better be finished with your list. The *whole* list."

"OK, OK. But you're really cruel. I wonder if boys go through this much agony every time they ask a girl out for a date?"

"They probably get used to it after a while."

"Maybe that's why so many kids like to go steady. You don't have to worry about anyone saying no."

"No more stalling, Maureen. Get back to work. I'll talk to you when you're done."

Maureen hung up, resigned to her fate. Then she leaned back against the wall, feet stretched out on the floor in front of her, and imagined herself refusing a date with every boy in her English class. It wasn't that easy to say no without sounding snobbish, she decided.

"Maureen, finish up your phone calls, OK?" her mother called up. "I have to do some calling tonight, too."

"OK, Mom. Just one more."

Just one more. That made it sound so easy. Climbing Mt. McKinley would be easier than that. Looking down at her hands, Maureen realized her palms were sweating. If only she'd called Jake first instead of saving him for last! But there was no avoiding it now. Her heart pounding, her fingers trembling, Maureen quickly dialed his number, which she'd memorized a half hour before. She held her breath as the phone rang.

"Hello?" a woman's voice answered.

"Oh, hello, I'm Maureen Meyer. Could I speak to Jake, please?"

"Who? Lorene?"

"No, Maureen."

She heard her call, "Jake, Noreen for you," and cringed.

"Hi, Jake, it's Maureen Meyer," she said as soon as he came to the phone.

"Oh, hi, *Maureen*. How are you—just back from a run?"

Maureen felt reassured. He sounded friendly, so obviously he wasn't mad at her for not talking to him.

"Not just back, although I did get a run in today. How's your big, beautiful dog?" *The one who almost bit me*, she added silently.

"Great," Jake replied. "You'll have to come by and see him again."

Maureen smiled. Then she realized he couldn't see that she was smiling. She had to say something—quick!

"Jake, I called to invite you to a party. Debbie's having a bunch of kids over for a pizza party next Saturday, and she asked me to help call the guests. Do you think you'll be able to come?"

"I hope I can. Just a minute, and I'll check it out."

Maureen held the line, praying the answer would be yes.

"No problem. I'll be there. Sounds like it'll be fun. Are you on the planning committee?"

"Yes, I'm helping Debbie with all the details."

"Do you think you could make sure there are a lot of anchovies on the pizza? I just discovered I love anchovies. Olives, too. I gotta have my pizza thick with them."

"I think we can arrange that. All pizza made to order. We're going to make them ourselves from scratch at Debbie's."

"Great. Do you know how to toss the dough up in the air and catch it on your fingertips? I used to watch my uncle Pete do it when I was a kid. He worked in a pizza place in New York. I was always pretty impressed with that."

"I don't think we'd better try it—unless you can show us, of course. If you have any other expert tips, though, let me know."

"Will do. Well, thanks a lot for inviting me. See you then."

Suddenly, Maureen was sorry that the conversation was ending. She'd been having such a good time, she'd forgotten to be nervous. "OK. 'Bye."

"Wait, Maureen. You forgot to tell me when. And what's Debbie's address?"

She quickly gave him the information, and a minute later, they hung up. *Done!* Maureen thought, feeling elated. And it hadn't been as bad as she'd thought it would be. Not bad at all.

Jake was so easy to talk to, she had almost forgotten what she had called for.

And he *was* coming to the party. *Hurray!* she thought, stretching her cramped muscles. Luck was on her side. Nothing could possibly keep things from working out now.

The dress. It was always so hard to find a dress when she needed one. Whenever she went window-shopping, she noticed a million terrific outfits. Of course when you don't actually try them on, you can imagine yourself looking terrific in every one. You're never disillusioned by the cruel facts.

Maureen had always been tall and slender, which shouldn't have been a problem where clothes were concerned. But things didn't always fall exactly where they were supposed to. It wasn't easy to lengthen pants that prominently displayed an ankle bone. The waistlines of some of her dresses were halfway up to her armpits. But larger sizes often left her with the shoulder seams drooping over her arms. Shopping for such an important outfit would be hard, she knew.

On Thursday when Debbie came over after school, they went upstairs, flopped down on Maureen's bed, and began thumbing through some recent issues of *Seventeen*. The Sunday newspaper ads piled on the floor hadn't produced any ideas, but the magazine looked more promising.

"Hey, Deb. Look at this. 'Twenty Tips for a Sexier Wardrobe,' page forty-eight. This is exactly what I need—a new image. Why not a sexier image?"

Feeling adventurous, Maureen turned to the page and skimmed the article as Debbie looked over her shoulder.

"These girls look sexy, all right."

"This jewelry is wild! Three earrings!"

"Wow, how about this one. All in black with a see-through lace blouse!"

"This striped caftan is an eye-catcher."

But after they'd both read the article carefully and examined the pictures critically, Maureen frowned. "I still don't know how to have a sexy wardrobe," she complained. "It's more the expression on their faces that makes them look sexy, not the clothes."

Standing up, she walked over to the mirror. "I think I'm just too wholesome looking."

"Yeah, you do sort of have a girl-next-door look," Debbie agreed.

Maureen tried a Brooke Shields pout—stuck out her chin, lowered her eyes, and thrust back one shoulder.

Debbie laughed. "I'm not sure if you look sexy or totally ridiculous," she teased.

Maureen pulled her hair straight back, put

on some dangling earrings, and affected her most sultry expression.

"This isn't right, either. I look like a little girl playing gypsy. I wish I could be in one of those makeup promotions where they make you over and take before-and-after pictures for a magazine. I definitely need professional help. Hey, wait a minute. I'm staring at all the help I need. Debbie, you're good with hair. Can you think of something dramatic? My everyday style is so . . . everyday."

"Well, let's experiment."

For the next hour Debbie combed and brushed, pulled and twisted, and curled and braided, finally coming up with a stunning combination of braids and curls.

"This is it!" Debbie announced triumphantly. "How do you like it, Madame?"

Maureen swallowed. She didn't want to hurt Debbie's feelings, but after all, she did want Jake to *recognize* her.

"Well, it's interesting, but . . . um . . . I don't think I could ever get it back like this again," Maureen replied, peering critically at her reflection. "Thanks for trying, Deb, but I think I'll stick with my old style for a while. We probably won't have an extra hour before the party to fix it this way again."

"I guess you're right," Debbie conceded. "You

have beautiful hair anyway. You don't need any-thing special."

"But I do still need a dress," Maureen moaned.

Mrs. Meyer called up the stairs. "Maureen, I'm ready to go to the mall."

"Be down in a minute."

Debbie gathered up her share of the maga-zines and newspapers, while Maureen combed out her hair.

"Good luck with your shopping," Debbie called out as she left. "Let me know if you find something."

As mother and daughter drove to the mall, Maureen was lost in thought.

"Why so quiet? Thinking about the party?"

"Yeah, sort of. We were trying to figure out what my new look should be, but we couldn't find one that seemed right."

"Hmmm, I sort of like your old look—pretty, nice, neat."

"Well, uh, I thought I'd try to look a little . . . sexier for the party. I want someone to notice me."

"Oh, I'm sure everyone will notice you. You're a very attractive girl. It's really personality that counts, anyway."

"Mom, I'm not so sure about that. I appreci-ate what you're trying to say, but everybody's parents think their kid looks good. I'm worry-ing about the more critical eyes of the American male teenager. According to this article I just read in *Seventeen*, you have to show off your figure and look sort of old and knowing."

"It said that?"

"Well, not exactly, but that's how the pictures looked."

"That's probably what you have to do to be a teenage model, but I don't know if it would make you more popular with the high school crowd."

Maureen was starting to feel frustrated. This was getting too hard to try to explain. "Anyway, I want to find something different—something really interesting that no one else could be wearing."

They pulled into the mall parking lot and began a long, tiring trek through the dress departments and boutiques.

Nothing seemed right.

"Mom, I can't look anymore," Maureen declared several hours later. She felt so exhausted, she wasn't sure she'd have the strength to reach into her purse and pull out her wallet. "My eyes won't even focus. It's too much. What'll I do?"

"I don't know, honey. This is a lot harder than I thought it would be. I think you've tried on everything in your size in the entire mall. You always used to be so easy to buy clothes for . . . when you looked like the girl next door, that is. I really don't know what you have in mind for this 'new look,' and I'm not sure you do, either. Let's go home. I've had it."

"Me, too. I can't stand the thought of trying on one more thing."

They walked back to the car on aching feet and drove home silently. As they were about to turn onto a side street, a new shop sign caught Maureen's eye: KATYA'S—FANCY CLOTHES OLD AND NEW FROM FAR AND WIDE. The clothing store was squeezed between an antique shop and a pet store. An odd assortment of items was displayed in the window: an old-fashioned white high-necked gown, a red-and-orange-flowered Hawaiian muumuu, a circular black felt skirt from the fifties with a pink poodle on it, and some one-of-a-kind party dresses by local designers.

"Mom, let's stop," she said impulsively. "There just might be something here. You never know what you'll find in a place like this."

Mrs. Meyer sighed as she pulled up in front of the shop.

The store was divided into tiny cubicles, each one decorated in the theme of a different era. Each decade had its corner, starting with the antique gowns and ending with a contemporary boutique. Along the front was an "Oriental bazaar." It was almost like a museum.

"Look at these, Maureen. Japanese kimonos."

"I couldn't dance or do anything much besides sit and look exotic in one of those."

"How about an Indonesian sarong? The bright colors and patterns are so pretty."

"What if it fell off? I don't see any buttons or zippers on them." Maureen looked a little longer before telling her mother, "This stuff is too weird. Let's look in the 'Eighties and Beyond' section."

She had almost decided to call it quits, when she saw the perfect dress. It was slate blue and luxurious to her touch. She had to try it on. If it didn't fit, she'd be heartbroken.

The dress hadn't been made in a traditional style, but it wasn't contemporary or trendy in any way either. Instead, it seemed to be a mixture of several different eras, created by someone with an eye for beauty and a passion for romance. The soft folds slithered over Maureen's shoulders, clung flatteringly around her hips, then flared out gracefully in a cascade of flowers hand painted in pastel hues.

"It's beautiful, isn't it," commented Katya, the owner of the shop, as Maureen emerged from the dressing room to model the dress for her mother. "This material is very special. It's hand painted in Korea. Look at the brush strokes. Very talented, the artist. Then we create the dress here in my studio."

"Yes, it's lovely," her mother added. "You look fantastic, Maureen. It's a perfect fit."

Katya chimed in again, "Just right for your coloring, too. Your complexion and hair color make you a 'spring,' you know. I advise all my 'springs' to buy these shades exclusively. They're so becoming.

"She's got the figure for it, too," she went on, turning to Mrs. Meyer. "You know," she said, "so many of the young girls these days, they can't wear my clothes. Too many Cokes, every day the potato chips . . ."

Maureen, feeling a little awkward with so much discussion of her appearance, slipped away to take off the dress. Then she noticed the price tag. She'd have to go into debt for it. But it would be worth it. She'd do anything to make Jake notice her. And he couldn't ignore her on Saturday night—not in that dress.

Five

Maureen thought her troubles were over. She threw herself into the preparations for the party with more enthusiasm than she'd felt in a long time. Her dad didn't even seem to mind that she wouldn't be seeing him till Sunday.

At last Saturday afternoon arrived. Maureen and Debbie sat on the floor of Maureen's room going through her record collection, trying to decide which ones to bring over to the party. The pile of "yes" records was much smaller than the pile of rejects.

"I don't know why I ever bought so many dumb albums," Maureen remarked self-consciously. "I can't stand most of them anymore."

"I know what you mean. I usually take my old ones to the Record Exchange. You can get rid of your duds by trading them. Of course, sometimes the new ones turn out to be even worse. But at least they're different."

"I wonder what kind of music Jake likes."

"Well, we'll find out soon enough. Hey, why don't you call him up and ask him to bring over a few of his favorite records?"

"Oh, no! You've got to be kidding. That first phone call almost did me in. I don't want to press my luck. I think I might be allergic to telephones. My skin feels all prickly even thinking about it."

"OK." Debbie laughed. "Calm down. I thought you were making progress, but I guess it takes time. We've got plenty of music. If worse comes to worst, we'll put on the radio."

"Come on, let's take this stuff over to your house—the sauce and everything—then I'll have to start getting ready. You know it takes forever for my hair to dry."

They walked the two short blocks between their houses several times before everything was arranged for the party, leaving Maureen with just enough time to get ready.

Because the evening was so special, Maureen took particular care with her preparations. She wanted to feel as glamorous as she hoped to look.

She washed her hair in the shower, then filled the tub for a nice, relaxing soak to calm her nerves. She leaned back, the towel wrapped around her head making a cushion against the hard rim of the tub. She closed her eyes as the water crept up to her chin. It felt good.

In her mind she went over the things she'd talk about with Jake: photography, of course; music; teachers—that was always good for a laugh. She'd ask him about his family. And his dog. Everyone loves to talk about his dog. What was his name? Max something. Maximillian. Pretty fancy name for a dog. She didn't care too much for big dogs, but she'd try to be open-minded about Max. He was probably a very nice dog once you got to know him.

When her hair was finally dry, her jewelry selected, and her makeup applied, Maureen slipped on the dress. She looked in the mirror for a long time, examining herself from every angle. She looked good. Maybe she could face this crowd, after all. She thought it was amazing how a dynamite dress could give her confidence.

Debbie was still setting all the food out on the kitchen counter when Maureen arrived. "I think we're going to have a great party, Mo. Doesn't all this look delicious?"

Then Debbie looked up. "Maureen, you look fantastic! That dress was worth every penny. You'll have to show me this Katya's place. It's a real find."

"Thanks," Maureen said, filled with happiness that her friend approved. "I knew you'd like it. You look great, too."

Debbie was wearing an old-fashioned lacy blouse and a long skirt—a subtly woven plaid of blues and browns. A gold-and-ivory brooch drew the eye to her pale face and the dark wispy curls that circled it.

"I got this outfit a couple of months ago, but this is the first chance I've had to wear it."

"It's really nice."

"There's one thing we're both going to have to watch out for, though."

"You mean too many boys asking us to dance?"

"Yeah, that and tomato sauce."

Maureen just laughed. She was feeling so good that night that she didn't think even a little tomato-sauce stain could dampen her spirits.

After they finished putting out the refreshments, the doorbell rang, and Maureen went down to the family room to put on some music. She was starting to feel nervous. She'd been down there a million times, but that time it felt strange—like a huge auditorium where she was about to perform. The comfortable sofa seemed more like a stage prop.

She didn't know any of the early arrivals very well, so she retreated to a corner to thumb through the record collection. Her hand started to tremble as she turned the album covers.

Debbie had a great collection. There were some advantages to having older sisters. You might have to wear hand-me-down clothes sometimes, but you also got a lot of hand-me-down records. Some of these "golden oldies" you would never be able to find in the stores anymore. She was getting down to some really ancient ones that must have belonged to Debbie's parents: old jazz tunes, a couple of Beatles albums, *Aretha Franklin's Greatest Hits.*

Maureen felt someone leaning over her shoulder and heard a male voice say "Hi." She shivered and turned around, startled. It was only Mike.

"Hey! Don't look so disappointed. Who were you expecting, Romeo?" Maureen blushed, mad at herself for giving away what she'd been thinking—that it was Jake who'd been leaning over her.

Mike started flipping through the albums, too. "Do you like blues? Taj Mahal is my favorite. I've learned some awesome songs off his records. Then I jazz up the arrangements a little, of course. Here, let's put on this Van Halen. That'll liven up the party a bit."

"I didn't know you played the guitar."

"Yeah, I've been playing for a few years. My band plays at school dances sometimes. You mean to say you never noticed me? I play lead."

"Well, no." Maureen didn't want to admit that she'd never been asked to a dance. She thought fast. "I guess the music was so good it outshone the players."

"Yeah, maybe. I'd hate to think my face was that forgettable, though. I'll never become a star that way." Mike pretended to frown, but his eyes still crinkled with humor.

Talking with Mike turned out to be surprisingly easy, and Maureen started to relax and enjoy herself. She felt like one of the gang at last. Mike was really sort of fun. They went back upstairs to get some snacks, and Mike amused her with the adventures of his band. She was laughing hysterically at his funny comments when she saw someone out of the corner of her eye and almost choked. Jake had arrived, and he was talking to Karen Rider, who had her arm playfully resting on his shoulder.

This wasn't how it was supposed to be! she thought, no longer listening to Mike's banter. Where was Karen's boyfriend? They had only invited her because she was going to bring along her own boyfriend. Now she'd gotten a head start on Maureen's. Well, Jake wasn't exactly hers, but . . .

"Maureen. Maureen . . . Boy, my jokes are really falling flat now. Come on, Maureen, you should be laughing. I just said something humorous!"

"Oh, sorry. I lost track of what you were saying for a minute. What was it?"

"Never mind," Mike said, looking a little

crushed. But Mike had sensed the change in her, and the mood between them was broken.

Maureen couldn't enjoy Mike's attention when Jake was with Karen. She strained to hear what they were saying and had trouble keeping up her end of the conversation with Mike. She kept looking at him and smiling, but her responses were wooden. Finally Mike made his excuses and went off to find a more receptive audience.

Maureen would rather have died than go up to Jake and Karen by herself, so she found her way over to Debbie, who was chattering with a group. She tried to stand so that she had a good view of the rest of the room.

Then without warning, all eyes were on her as one of the girls broke in, "Here she is, Miss America. We've been waiting to get a look at that fancy dress of yours, Maureen. Debbie told us you'd be a knockout."

Although the words were nice, her tone of voice was not, and Maureen had no idea how to reply. She started to blush. Fortunately, Debbie came to her rescue.

"You all just wish you'd seen it first," she said, trying to get everyone back into a good mood. Maureen looked back over at Jake.

He and Karen had been sitting around a table in the corner of the kitchen. Daffodils in a blue vase reflected the yellow-and-blue pattern of the wallpaper of the surrounding alcove, and a few candles on the table made Jake's dark eyes sparkle in the warm light. He looked very handsome.

Maureen liked the way his hands looked, too: long and slender. He was reaching out for the vase, turning it around to examine the glaze, a fine network of crackles under a translucent blue-green. His fingers looked like a musician's— a violinist's, maybe. They were long and tapered, but strong. How could Mike play a guitar with his hands, she wondered. His short stubby fingers looked as if they'd always be pushing one another off the strings.

Out of the corner of her eye, she saw Karen leave Jake's side and head for the bathroom. She felt a wave of fear. That was it. She had to make her move right then.

Maureen walked over to the newly vacated chair next to Jake and plopped down. She audibly let out her breath and realized with horror that she had been holding it as she made her way across the room. She must remember to breathe. It was hard enough to make casual conversation without having to gasp for breath between sentences.

"Hi, Jake," she said softly. "Have you been here long? I didn't see you come in."

"Oh, not too long. I had to finish up some prints I was working on before I could get over, but I finally made it. Nice party, isn't it?"

"Yeah, nice. There's music downstairs."

"Mm-hmm. I can hear it. Want to grab a couple of Cokes and go down?"

"OK."

As they headed downstairs, Maureen noticed Karen reenter the room and couldn't help feeling a little self-satisfied as she saw her scowling at Jake's empty chair.

The noise level down in the family room was a little more than she had bargained for. The second side of the Van Halen album was still playing, and someone had turned the volume up full blast. They stood against the wall drinking and watching the other kids dance for a while. The music was too loud for conversation. *Just as well*, thought Maureen.

As she sipped her Coke, she tried to figure out if she should drink it fast or slow. As long as they were drinking, Jake would probably be content to stand and watch and wouldn't ask her to dance. But if she drank it up quickly and he still didn't want to dance, she'd have to stand there with an empty glass and nothing to do. She decided to keep her glass at the same level as Jake's. Then they'd both be at loose ends at about the same time.

It worked. As soon as she set her empty glass down, Jake added his to it, took her by the hand, and said, "Let's dance."

He was a wonderful dancer and seemed to

know just what he was doing. Then someone changed the record, and the dancing turned slow. Before Maureen had a chance to get nervous, Jake pulled her close to him.

Maureen felt a flush of heat, and her breath caught in her throat. Her head swam, and she felt slightly giddy, all trembly and fluttery inside. Jake's body was warm, and he smelled nice. A minute later she relaxed enough to lean her head comfortably against his shoulder, and she was rewarded by the feel of his arm reaching more tightly around her waist. All at once, Maureen felt happier than she ever had before. Dancing in Jake's arms was everything she had wanted it to be. If only the music would never end.

Someone did, however, change the record, and when the fast music started again, Maureen began to loosen up. She loved dancing, loved the movement and the beat. When she was little, she'd taken both ballet and tap lessons, going to classes several times a week, right through eighth grade. When she started high school, though, it had suddenly seemed like too much. She gave up her lessons rather than search for a new teacher, but she still enjoyed dancing every chance she got.

The heavy beat drove her worries away. You needed a partner to get on the floor, but after that you were on your own. The floor grew crowded with couples, and soon everything was forgotten but the music. Maureen didn't try to show off, but she did attract attention. The other dancers stopped to watch, and Maureen didn't even notice. When the music stopped, she was exhilarated.

Suddenly a few kids started to clap, and Maureen looked up, surprised. People were smiling encouragingly, and she smiled back. Then she noticed Karen, who had also been watching them dance.

"That was quite a performance, Maureen. Now come on upstairs, Jake. I've fixed that pizza you ordered."

"But I didn't . . ."

"No 'buts'! It's all ready—heavy on the anchovies, just the way you like it. Hurry, or it'll get cold."

Pushing past Maureen, Karen propelled Jake back upstairs for pizza.

She's kidnapped him, Maureen thought to herself when she'd recovered her wits. She was in shock. Karen had whisked him away so fast, neither she nor Jake had had time to protest. One minute she was in heaven, the next she was back where she'd started, trying—not too successfully—to figure out how the girl-gets-boy game worked. Obviously, rule number one was that you could never let your guard down for a single minute.

Discouraged, Maureen sat down on the sofa and watched the other dancers for a while. She wanted to dance some more, but partners were getting scarce. What had happened to all those extra boys Debbie had promised? They sure weren't downstairs.

She realized that the party had started to break up into pairs and small groups. But somehow Maureen had missed out—like arriving for a game a few minutes after the teams had been chosen. Before she had started dancing with Jake, it had been a large mixable group, but now everyone seemed settled in various corners, laughing at private jokes. Aside from a few dancers, she couldn't catch anyone's eye. She saw only groups of backs clumped around the edges of the room.

She decided to stay put in hopes that someone else would ask her to dance. It was a long wait. Maybe the boys who weren't confident dancers were scared off by her celebrity status—not wanting to put themselves in the limelight. Either that or there must be some other reason why everyone was avoiding her. Maybe her face had turned blue or sprouted pimples or something. Perhaps it was time for a trip up to the bathroom to see if she looked funny.

Maureen wished with all her heart that she could quietly slip away and go home. But that was out. She had promised to stay and help clean up after the party.

Come on, don't be a wimp, she told herself. *Prove to yourself and to everyone else that you can fit in.* She'd have to stick it out. After reassuring herself in the bathroom that she still looked normal, she went upstairs to the kitchen, planning to help with the pizzas. Probably not all the kids wanted to make their own, anyway. At least that would give her something to do.

Jennifer and Kevin were standing near the counter with a rolling pin and a big glob of dough looking helpless. "Hey, Maureen," they called out to her. "How about giving us a hand over here? This stuff is too sticky."

"I've had almost four years of home ec., and I don't have a clue," Jennifer said. "Look, every time I roll one side out it shrinks back up again before I can get to the other side."

"Don't worry, I'll handle it," Maureen offered, brightly. "I think all you need is a little more flour on everything. I'll fix the dough, and you two can take over from there."

"Thanks. We were afraid we'd faint from hunger before we could get that dough flattened out."

Pausing to scrounge around for a big apron in the pantry, Maureen joined them at the counter and was kept busy rolling out crusts for about ten more pizzas.

"You're pretty good at this," Kevin commented as he sprinkled the last bit of cheese on his creation.

"I guess you could say I'm on a roll," Maureen quipped, and they all laughed.

See, it's not so hard to talk to these people, Maureen told herself as she removed her floury apron. While she still didn't know Kevin and Jennifer well, she felt a lot closer to them than she had before the party.

So who needs Jake? Maureen thought. But as she poured herself a Coke at the snack table, she glanced around the room. Outside the kitchen, she saw a bunch of kids sitting on the back stairs talking. But he wasn't there, either. Better check out the family room. He couldn't have left already. It wasn't even eleven. She had been hoping for a chance to get Jake away from Karen.

Halfway down the stairs she could see all the couples in the family room. There was Karen, dancing with Alex now, but no Jake. Mike came down the stairs and stood next to her.

"Mike," Maureen began, thinking she probably owed him an explanation for her abrupt behavior. "Hey, I'm sorry I couldn't concentrate on what you were saying before. I was just preoccupied with something."

"That's all right. It wasn't a great story, anyway. How about dancing?"

"Great. I'd really like to."

Her plans for Jake had fallen through, but at least she could dance. The evening wouldn't be a total loss.

And it wasn't. Maureen found herself having a surprisingly good time. She was even more surprised when she looked around and found that suddenly most of the guests had gone. At last everyone had said good-bye. It was after midnight, and only Maureen and Debbie were left: Maureen rinsing out soda bottles and piling them into large bags for the refund, while Debbie wiped the counter and put away the leftovers.

"Well, Mo, what do you think? Pretty awesome party, wasn't it? Everyone seemed to be having a good time."

"It was terrific, Deb. You ought to be proud of yourself." Then a sigh escaped Maureen's lips.

"What's the matter, Maureen? Didn't *you* have a good time? You looked like you were having fun. I saw how you sneaked Jake away from Karen. That was a cool move. Couldn't have done better myself."

All of her good feelings vanished in an instant. Setting down a soda bottle with a whack, Maureen looked over at Debbie. "But she snatched him right back, and he just went with her.

And *she* made him his anchovies and olive pizza. I was supposed to do that. Nothing worked out the way I had planned it."

"Well, you can't take these little setbacks too hard. You had some bad luck, that's all. Karen told me Brian was grounded for the week, so she came by herself."

"We should never have invited her in the first place. She shouldn't have tried to monopolize Jake just because Brian couldn't come."

"You can't blame her for trying."

"But did he have to go along with it so easily? That's what bugs me. We were having a great time dancing, in she comes, and *zap*, he's gone. That was the last I saw of him."

"Just don't get discouraged. You shouldn't have stopped trying just because he ate Karen's pizza. I doubt if he's really interested in her— he's a friend of her brother's, that's all."

But Maureen wouldn't be comforted.

"We hardly got to talk at all. I had all these interesting things I was going to say, and now they're wasted."

"Wasted!" Debbie exclaimed, laughing. "What do you mean, wasted? You'll see him again. Just write them down and save them for another time."

"They'll sound funny then. I'll have to think up new stuff."

"Jake's a very popular guy, you know—so you

have to expect a little competition. I bet he enjoys all the attention he's been getting lately. Come on now, let's finish up. I'm exhausted, but Mom said I could never have another party unless we left the kitchen spotless."

The party had been a success, but her attempts to talk to Jake had been a dismal failure. Next time, Maureen vowed to herself, no one was going to interfere with her plans.

Six

On Monday, Maureen's English teacher, Mr. Devon, asked Mike and her to stop by after school.

"Wonder what he wants?" Mike whispered as they filed out of the classroom.

"Do you think we're in trouble?" Maureen replied, feeling uneasy. "My homework hasn't been very good lately, especially on Mondays. It's always hard to get everything done when I spend the weekend in Cambridge. If we have a busy weekend, I leave some of it for the trolley ride home, but I can't concentrate if the train is crowded."

"I've handed in everything on time. I don't think it's about our homework. It must be something else."

"We'll find out after school, I guess," Maureen said stoically as she went upstairs to French and Mike continued down the hall to the gym.

She was still a little apprehensive as she

walked into the empty English classroom after the last period. Mr. Devon wasn't the kind of teacher kids chatted with after school. He was a good teacher, but distant, and he seemed a little scary. He was totally involved in his subject, and she couldn't imagine him at home, joking around with a family or doing anything other than reading or discussing books.

Mike walked in a few minutes after she did. He didn't look worried at all, Maureen noticed. She would have to learn to stop expecting the worst.

"Hi, kids," Mr. Devon said as he joined them. "Thanks for stopping by. I won't keep you long. Say, I saw you out running the other day, Maureen. You sure make it look easy. How far do you go?"

"Oh, about four or five miles, I guess."

"Well, keep it up. Going to enter any races? I think there's a big one that goes along the Charles River in the fall."

"Maybe I will," she answered, smiling.

"Well, to get down to business. You may know that one of my classes is English as a second language. ESL, we call it. You may also be aware of the fact that a number of new foreign students arrived midsemester this year, and they've been having a particularly hard time of it. As a result, I'm trying to start a tutoring program for those foreign students who need extra help, and I thought you two would be good candidates. I'm asking a few of my best students to volunteer to be English tutors during their free periods."

"I'm afraid I don't know anything about teaching English, Mr. Devon," Mike spoke up, voicing Maureen's sentiments exactly.

"That's OK. You *do* speak the language. There'll be two training sessions after school to show you some techniques. After that we'll meet just once or twice to see how everyone's doing," Mr. Devon continued, acting as if they really didn't have a choice.

"School will be over before we get the hang of it," Mike put in.

"We *are* getting started very late this year, but I'm hoping you'll be able to do it next year, too. We'll give you all some credits to make it worth your while. It should be fun, too. I have a really interesting group this year—worth getting to know. How about you, Maureen? Can I count on you?"

Maureen felt a surge of pride. It was quite a compliment to be asked, but she hoped she'd be able to do it. She hated to disappoint people. "Ummmm. Sure."

"And you, Mike?"

"OK, as long as it's during school. I work after school most days, and my band rehearses every weekend."

"Good, I think you'll get a lot out of it," Mr. Devon replied, looking very pleased. "The foreign students are very nice, once you get to know them. Our first training session will be on Thursday at two-fifteen. Bring a notebook and folder for some information I'll be handing out. Thanks for signing up," he said as he added their names to his list. "See you Thursday."

As soon as she walked out the door, Maureen's doubts resurfaced.

"I wish I didn't always agree to things so quickly," she confided to Mike. "How can you help someone speak English when you don't know their language? All I know is a little French, and I'm sure the students he has in mind aren't French."

"No, they're probably Asian."

"It must be almost impossible to learn a language by just listening. I had plenty of trouble learning French, even with Madame Marceau repeating the words a million times and a book to study from."

"I didn't even take French."

"I guess it's too late to back out now. Mr. Devon'll think I'm unreliable." Mike just smiled.

"See you on Thursday, then. 'Bye, Maureen."

" 'Bye." *Mike is such an easygoing guy,* Maureen thought. *He seems to take everything in stride. Well, at least that's one other tutor I'll know.*

Getting involved would probably be good for her, she decided. She hadn't been doing much during her free period, anyway. She usually went to the library, but lately she'd been spending most of it daydreaming about Jake.

She imagined herself walking home from school with him, laughing easily, talking about important things, going to the movies. Maureen had never been to the movies with a boy, but she had no trouble imagining herself snuggled up to Jake in the dim theater. He'd hold her hand gently—his palms would never sweat, Maureen was certain—and feed her buttery popcorn with his long, sensitive fingers. Maureen shivered with delight just imagining it. They'd do everything and go everywhere together. Her weekends would be filled with dates and parties, and after school they would study together.

Maybe she'd help him in his darkroom. That could be very cozy—except for all those smelly chemicals. On second thought, she'd leave the developing to Jake and just accompany him on assignments with more romantic possibilities, like boating on the Charles or going on a fall-foliage tour.

It started to take her longer and longer to complete her homework assignments. She could hardly get through a paragraph without stopping at least once to wonder what Jake might be doing at that moment. She looked up from her work frequently to see if by any chance he had come to the library or was passing by in the halls.

On Thursday Maureen went to Mr. Devon's room and was surprised to find it almost full. Mr. Devon was a terrific recruiter. She wasn't the only one who couldn't say no. He had cleverly appealed to their pride by saying he was only asking his best students. Glancing around, Maureen saw that the few seats left were in the front row. As she made her way to an empty desk, she caught a glimpse of someone in the corner, and her heart jumped. She couldn't believe it. It was Jake Harmon.

From that moment on Maureen had trouble concentrating on the lecture. Mr. Devon's instructions on how to teach English simply went in one ear and out the other. Fortunately, however, he had everything written down. She could study his work sheets later. Maureen glanced back at Jake from time to time to make sure he was really there. He was entertaining the kids in the back with humorous comments that Maureen couldn't quite hear, but he smiled a friendly hello when she caught his eye.

Soon the meeting was over, and she stood in line to get her assignment.

"Your student is Trang Thi Lah, Maureen," explained Mr. Devon. "She'll meet with you in the library during fourth period. Trang just arrived last week, so she doesn't speak much English. Look at the section in your notes about how to begin, and if you have any questions, let me know at our session tomorrow, OK?"

"OK," she replied. She rushed out of the room, hoping to catch sight of Jake, but he and his friends were already far down the hall.

Maureen was one of the first ones there for the second session. She took a seat by the window where she could keep an eye on the door. When Jake came in, she looked up and smiled. He was wearing a faded plaid shirt with the sleeves rolled up. His arms looked strong and brown. She liked the way she walked, his tall, lanky body moving with a kind of unconscious grace. Coming over, he flopped his books on the desk next to hers, and Maureen's heart soared.

"Hi, Maureen, who'd you get?" he asked.

"I got a Vietnamese girl. Doesn't know a word of English."

"Mine's from Japan. Her father's a scientist or something."

"You got a girl?"

"Yeah." Jake smiled mischievously. "I told old Devon I wouldn't do it unless I got a beautiful girl."

Maureen was a little taken aback by his comment, but she realized he was probably teasing, so she plunged on. "I haven't met mine yet. I need to get a lot of stuff together and make some flash cards first. According to Devon, visual aids are important for beginners."

"Sounds like we could both use some help. Want to get together after the meeting? If you tell me what to do, I'm terrific at cutting and pasting. My kindergarten teacher always said I was the greatest!"

"Well . . ." Maureen hesitated. She was supposed to go to Cambridge after school. But she could leave a message on her dad's answering machine explaining that she'd be over later. If Jake was the impulsive type, she would be, too! Maureen smiled, delighted. "I'd love some help. I've got some projects started at my house, if you want to come over for a while."

"OK. Sounds good to me."

Mr. Devon spent almost an hour explaining the different methods you could use to teach English, but Maureen heard even less of that meeting than the previous one. She hoped Jake was paying attention.

She wondered if he thought about her as much as she thought about him. Not likely. Boys never seemed to care as much. But why was that? Were they simply less emotional, or was it conditioning by society? If only she had a brother or two to study, then Maureen was sure she'd know more about how boys thought.

As they walked to her house after the meeting, Maureen was anything but introspective. She could hardly believe what was happening— she was walking home from school with a boy! She felt as if she had enough energy to run ten marathons, and holding her head a little higher, she found herself chatting away as if she did this all the time.

"Debbie's party was fun, wasn't it?" Jake asked. "Too bad I had to leave early. I was hoping we could do some more dancing."

"Me, too. I was wondering where you went. How come you had to leave?"

"I had an emergency call from my editor. Some photos I had submitted to the *Gazette* the day before were accidentally damaged at the printer's, so I had to get a new set over to them by eight o'clock the next morning. I stayed up half the night redoing them."

"Oh, wow, you must be exhausted," Maureen declared.

"No, not at all," Jake said. Then, looking at her mischievously, he beat his chest with his hands and gave a little Tarzan-like yell. "Me no feel pain when around pretty girl like you." And in spite of herself, Maureen laughed.

They went in the front door of Maureen's old Victorian house and entered a large oak-paneled hallway. Passing through the living room, Maureen dumped her books on the coffee table, tossed her sweater on the sofa, and deposited her shoes near the door. The room was inviting and comfortable looking, but it didn't really seem lived in. In spite of deliberate efforts at giving it her personal stamp, it looked as if a photographer for *Better Homes and Gardens* was expected at any minute.

"Come into the dining room, Jake. I have my stuff spread out on the table there."

There was a large pile of magazines and old Sears catalogues already spread out on the table from the night before. She had been cutting out pictures of watches, fans, radios, and other things and pasting them on three-by-five cards.

"Looks like you've been busy," Jake remarked as he saw the clutter of paper, scissors, and magazines scattered over the table.

She put him to work immediately. "You can continue what I've been doing here—going through this catalogue and cutting. This pile is for objects. I'm pasting one on one side of the card and two or more on the other to teach plurals. This pile is for descriptive words like fat, thin, happy. The last pile is for activities. Miscellaneous is over here."

"Maureen," her mother called out from her office, "I didn't expect you this afternoon. Aren't you going to your dad's?"

"Yes, but I've got some stuff I have to do first," she answered. "I'll call him in a minute to let him know I'll be coming late."

Her mother emerged from her office, neat and businesslike in her "work clothes," a beige suit and silk blouse.

"Mom, this is my friend Jake," Maureen said proudly. "He's teaching English, too, and we're going to make flash cards."

"Hi, Jake. Nice to meet you. Thanks for giving Maureen a hand." Then, turning to her daughter, Mrs. Meyer added, "I just made an appointment to show a house in Chestnut Hill at five-thirty. I didn't plan on your being here for dinner, so you'll just have to see what you can find in the fridge if you get hungry."

"That's OK, Mom. I'll eat something when I get to Dad's."

The phone rang, and Mrs. Meyer disappeared back into her office. Suddenly Maureen realized she should offer her guest something to eat. Boys were always supposed to be hungry, weren't they?

"I'll see if I can find us a snack, Jake. Don't get your hopes up, though. Mom's on a diet."

Maureen went into the kitchen and returned with a couple of apples and a dish of raw carrots on a tray with two glasses of skim milk.

Jake looked a little disappointed. "I'm desperate. I'll take it. Isn't your mother the cookie-baking type?"

"Afraid not. She claims her doctor won't allow her to bake. Health reasons."

"You all look pretty healthy to me. Does your whole family jog?"

"No, just my dad and me. He's really good. He was a track star in college. He quit for a while, but then he took it up again a few years ago. He taught me all the warm-up exercises and everything when I got started."

Maureen ripped out pages from magazines as she talked, placing them in piles in front of Jake for him to cut.

"It's nice you can spend so much time with your dad," Jake said. "My dad's out of town a lot. He's a lawyer and has to go down to New York or Washington a couple of times a month."

"I was afraid when my parents split up that I'd never see my dad again—that he'd move to Tahiti or someplace."

"You're lucky. Cambridge isn't that far."

"No, but it *would* be more fun to visit by sailboat than on the *T*."

"But think how depressing it would be to have to come back to school on Monday after spending the weekend in Tahiti."

"That would be hard. From parkas to bikinis and back to parkas again."

"At least they didn't send you off to boarding school," Jake added.

"Oh, no. They'd never do that."

"That's what happened to me when my parents were having trouble. I could never figure out why I had to go away. It seemed as if they were doing the fighting, but I was getting punished. Boy, I hated that school."

Boarding school! That was interesting, Maureen thought. And yet he'd decided to come back. "Where was it?"

"Up in New Hampshire. I came home on weekends, but only one parent at a time was ever around. It was as though the other one didn't exist." Maureen's heart went out to Jake. She knew how terrible she felt when her parents weren't getting along. *But Jake's parents had stayed together,* she thought with a pang.

"Well, at least they didn't get divorced."

"No, not yet. I think they called a temporary truce. That's when I started getting interested in photography. When I spent the entire day in the darkroom, I could forget that my parents weren't speaking to each other."

"How'd you figure out how to do all that developing stuff?"

"Oh, I read a lot of books and had some pretty good teachers. I did good work for my age—won a national contest when I was thirteen."

"It's neat to be really good at something, isn't it? I'd like to be a top runner someday."

"I've been thinking it might be good for me to ease up a little. I spend so much time on photography that I don't have much social life anymore."

Jake's comment surprised Maureen. How could anyone think of easing up on something he was so talented at? She'd have just the opposite reaction—to plunge even more seriously into the hobby, to work at it until she was as good as she could possibly be! Plus, Jake seemed to have more friends than almost anyone she knew.

"Jake! No social life? I don't believe it! You're one of the most popular kids in the school!"

"Yeah, everybody knows me, and I can talk and joke around easily with everybody. . . ." Jake was silent for a moment. "But you know, I'm not sure if I have a single really good friend that I can count on! If you don't play sports, it's hard to find good buddies." At that moment, more than anything, Maureen wanted to reach over and touch Jake, to brush aside the lock of soft brown hair that had fallen across his forehead.

"I'm lucky to have found Debbie," Maureen confided softly. "Or she found me, rather. I was so depressed when I moved here, about my parents, and about moving away from my friends and everything that I practically flunked out my first semester. My counselor asked Debbie to help me out, and we've been friends ever since."

"Yeah, Debbie's a great kid," Jake said warmly.

"I wouldn't have made it through without her."

Jake smiled and, picking up his apple, took a bite. "We'd better get cracking if you want to make it over to your dad's," he pointed out.

The cards they made became more and more outrageous. Jake had pasted a picture of Garfield onto a broccoli quiche. "The cat is on the quiche!" he quipped.

"How about this one? The woman is washing the elephant," Maureen said as she pasted a smiling young housewife with a bottle of liquid cleanser next to a huge, dusty elephant.

"I like that. Here's another one. The baby is sitting on a big cookie."

"How about—Superman is carrying a pizza?" Maureen was cutting out part of a Papa Gino's ad to put on the superhero's outstretched arms.

For the next two hours Maureen was in heaven. Working beside Jake could make anything seem fun—even cutting out pictures from old magazines.

Finally as he was gathering up his things to leave, Jake asked casually, "Are you ever around on weekends?"

"Sure," she lied, even though she couldn't think of one weekend in the last few months that she hadn't spent with her father. But Jake didn't say the magical words, "Will you go out with me?" And Maureen told herself she shouldn't expect too much too soon.

" 'Bye. Thanks for the help," she called, watching as Jake walked jauntily down the sidewalk, turning to wave as he reached the corner.

As soon as he was out of sight, Maureen raced back inside and grabbed the telephone. She couldn't wait another second to tell someone.

"Debbie, he just left!"

"Who? When? What's happening?"

"Jake! Jake came over after school today. We worked on tutoring projects, and he just left. I can't believe it. I think he likes me. He asked to work together all by himself, I didn't ask him or even drop a hint!"

"That's great, Mo! You sound like you had a good time. Your luck is changing fast. Didn't I tell you that you could accomplish almost anything once you put your mind to it?"

After giving Debbie a minute-by-minute account of the afternoon, about which she had total recall, Maureen hung up and then gave the room a superficial straightening before heading for the trolley station. She wondered if she should mention Jake again to her dad. She couldn't say she had a boyfriend yet. She couldn't even call this Friday afternoon a date.

In fact, there was nothing romantic about it at all except the way her heart pounded when their hands accidentally touched—and the way her spirits soared when he smiled at her. She decided to wait until she had something more concrete to report.

Maureen spent most of the weekend in her dad's apartment, cutting up his old magazines to finish her flash cards and gathering together objects and pictures of varying sizes, shapes, and colors in a big cardboard box to teach adjectives. Her dad was busy grading term papers, but he did find time to give her a few pointers on successful teaching methods. So by the end of the weekend, not only did Maureen feel prepared, but she also found herself looking forward to her first session with Trang.

On Monday Maureen hurried to the library during her free period, clutching her notebook and a big bag of visual aids for her lesson. Pausing at the library door, she looked quickly around the room. She scanned the tables for someone who might be Trang, hoping she would recognize her.

Then someone caught her eye—a tiny, frail-looking black-haired girl sitting at a table in the back. Some books were piled in front of her, but she wasn't reading. She just sat quietly, hands folded on her lap, staring down at them.

Maureen knew that must be her student, but

she didn't go in right away. Suddenly she wished she had never signed up for this. How could she possibly teach this person anything? How could she explain what the words meant if the girl couldn't understand what she was saying? Or what if *she* couldn't understand Trang's accent? Or if Trang didn't answer at all? Panic began to set in, until suddenly Maureen remembered how scared and unsure of herself she'd been at the party. But she'd pushed herself that night to plunge right in, and she'd actually had a pretty good time. She just had to learn to keep pushing herself.

Ok, here we go, Maureen thought, walking into the room. She crossed over to Trang and sat down beside her student at the table.

"Hi. Are you Trang? I'm Maureen, your tutor."

"Good afternoon. My name is Trang. How are you?" she answered formally.

"Fine, thanks. How are you?"

"I'm fine, thank you." Then silence.

Boy, she really is hard to understand, Maureen thought. Trang's voice was high-pitched and nasal, barely audible above the squeaking chairs and rustling papers around them. But at least Trang knew a little English. It was a start.

"Well, let's begin," Maureen said, hoping she didn't sound as worried as she felt.

Trang looked worried enough for both of them together. She looked terrified, in fact.

Opening her folder, Maureen took out several cards with pictures of people pasted on them. They went through the stack together, Maureen pointing to a picture, naming the action, and Trang repeating everything after her.

The rest of the period went quickly. Maureen pulled out more cards, and through a variety of methods—pictures sketched on paper, a little pantomime, and hand signals—she and Trang communicated. By the end of the period, Trang seemed to be getting the hang of it; she was even smiling a little. Maureen felt exhausted, but she also felt as if she had accomplished something. And, she had to admit, it had been fun.

She was glad she hadn't quit. It would have been crazy to give up the one thing she had in common with Jake, no matter how hard it was. Funny, no matter what activity she was doing or who she was with, her thoughts always came back to Jake. *If this is what love is like*, Maureen thought, *I'm lucky to have escaped it so far. If I'd fallen for someone any earlier, I might never have graduated from junior high!*

Seven

That night Maureen dreamed she was running. She was racing barefoot on a path through the woods, laughing and keeping just ahead of a young man struggling to catch up. She was teasing him and tempting him by staying just out of reach, smiling back at him over her shoulder. In the dream Maureen looked back and saw that it was Jake running behind her, his dark hair curling with sweat, grinning confidently as he clutched three golden fruits to his chest.

It was like the story of Atalanta that her father used to read her from her big book of Greek myths. As a child she had loved those wonderfully gory stories of gods and heroes and had begged to hear them read over and over again. One of her favorites had been the one about Atalanta, a princess who would only marry someone who could beat her in a race. One clever suitor threw down golden apples as they ran. She stopped to pick them up, lost the race, and gained a husband.

Sometimes dreams can give you good ideas, she thought as she dressed for school that morning. Maybe she could convince Jake to take up running. That way they'd have something in common, something they could do together on weekends and in the afternoons. On the way to school Maureen discussed it with Debbie.

"Listen, Mo, he's not the athletic type. If he wanted to spend his free time huffing and puffing around town, he'd be doing it already. He wouldn't need an invitation from you."

"But we could run together—I'd inspire him. It's a lot more fun to run with a partner than by yourself."

"Look how well I've resisted your efforts," Debbie countered. "You've been after me for ages, but luckily my strength of character has prevailed. I've carefully preserved my ladylike image and still can't run more than half a block without collapsing. And I'm proud of it."

"Well, not everyone's proud of being a physical wreck," Maureen retorted, hurt that Debbie didn't think her idea was a good one. "I bet he's just waiting for someone to help him get started."

"You never can tell. Maybe the thought of having you as a coach will make him jump at the chance. You can't underestimate the power of love," Debbie teased.

"Just because you hate running doesn't mean Jake will. It's *very* popular. We could even enter races together—like the town road race next fall."

"Remember, Mo, you're such a strong runner, he'd have to train awfully hard to keep up with you in an eight-mile race. Maybe he wouldn't mind if you were faster, but a lot of boys are sensitive about things like that."

"I bet he *doesn't* get much exercise."

"He's definitely on the thin side."

"But that's good," Maureen said. "Most top runners are thin and lanky—strong but thin."

"Jake doesn't look too strong, either. He probably never lifts anything heavier than a camera or a couple of books."

Maureen thought of all the time they'd have to spend together so she could coach him. "Well, he'll be a new man when I'm finished with him," she predicted.

"Maureen, you really *are* a dreamer."

As she walked home from school that afternoon, Maureen planned her strategy. She still believed that getting Jake interested in running was a great idea, no matter what Debbie said. It would bring them together in the most natural way possible. The more she thought about it, the more she liked it.

She'd start him off really slowly, just once or twice around the reservoir. It was only a mile.

Anyone who was breathing should be able to do that much. After a few weeks, they'd take some runs down by the Charles River. Then she would invite him up to Cambridge to meet her dad, and they'd all run together at Fresh Pond. Afterward they would cook up a big Chinese dinner in the wok. She was sure Jake and her dad would get along great.

As she opened the front door, she heard the TV. It was Mrs. Meyer in shorts and an old T-shirt, bouncing and stretching to a disco beat along with Jane Fonda. They had a tape of her exercise program and played it on their VCR. The routine seemed to have done quite a bit for Jane and her crew, but Mrs. Meyer was still a little too plump in the wrong places.

"Mom, why don't you stop all this and get some real exercise for a change," Maureen said with the conviction of a true believer. "You need some fresh-air aerobics, not just a few minutes of shuffling your feet around indoors."

"You may be right, but this suits me," her mother gasped between bends. "Running isn't good for everyone, you know. I don't think my knees could take all that pounding on the pavement. Also, I like a little privacy when I bounce around."

"Oh, Mom, nobody pays any attention. Everyone's so used to seeing runners, they don't notice anything."

"Well, Jane and I are doing just fine. You'll have to find another running mate."

"That's just what I'm going to do," Maureen called out confidently as she sailed into her room to change.

This time Maureen headed straight for the reservoir. She ran past Jake's house, an impressive-looking brick structure, three stories high, fronted by several tall white columns on either side of the door. She stared at the house as she went by, trying to figure out if Max had had his walk yet. The only person she saw was a gardener trimming a hedge in back.

Well, I'm going to keep running around that pond till he comes over, she thought. *I'll do ESP on him. No, not ESP. What is it when you make something move by thinking about it? Psychokinesis—that's what I'll do. I'll concentrate on getting him to come out here, and the power of my mind will make him appear.*

She was on her fourth turn around the pond and was starting to lose faith in her psychic powers when she saw a tall, lanky figure in jeans leading a large German shepherd onto the path at the far end. At last! This was working out perfectly; Maureen just knew she couldn't lose that day.

But as she sprinted down to meet them, Jake's good looks suddenly made her feel weak in the knees. He had on a sea-blue wind-

103

breaker that contrasted nicely with his deeply set brown eyes. He raised a hand in greeting.

"Hi," she called out, giving him her most dazzling smile.

"Hey, it's the speed demon! How're you doing? It's time for old Max's exercise. Want to join us?" Jake answered.

"Sure," Maureen replied, and they began walking. "You know, I've been thinking, Jake, you could probably use some exercise, too. Ever think of taking up running?"

"Well, no. I . . ."

"I could help you get started. It's really not hard at all if you start slowly."

"I don't think . . ."

"It would be a lot of fun to run together. Maybe we could even enter some races," she continued, her words coming faster and faster.

"Mmmm." Jake seemed uncomfortable. "You make it sound fun, but"—he looked down at Max—"I've never been much of a runner."

"That's all right. No one's good when they just start, but you'll pick it up in no time. I know you'll just love it. Come on, give it a try!" Maureen coaxed. Jake couldn't turn her down! He just couldn't. She had to make him say yes. Once he agreed to join her, the rest would be easy.

"I *would* like spending the time with you, Maureen, but I really can't run."

"Now, don't say *can't*. My dad says everyone can do it if they just use a little willpower."

"Maureen, I . . ."

"Look, you're already wearing running shoes. You're all set. Max will love it, too. Just give it a try," Maureen pleaded. "Once. Please. If you really hate it, I won't bug you anymore."

She realized she was begging him, but she couldn't stop herself. She'd put herself on the line, and he was about to refuse. She'd only asked him to try it once, but he probably thought she was being too pushy. He'd helped her one afternoon, and now she was planning his activities for every day of the week. She could understand why he was backing off.

Her crestfallen expression had an effect on Jake.

"OK, Maureen. I'll try it once. But you'll see. I'm really not a runner."

Maureen's good spirits returned immediately. She practically clapped her hands.

Jake had on his running shoes, so he was all set. They could begin right away. "OK, follow me," she called out.

This was her fifth lap, so she thought she'd set a nice easy pace for Jake, quite a bit slower than she had done the first four. As they rounded the first curve, Jake was breathing pretty hard. She slowed down a little.

"See, it's not so bad, is it?"

Jake didn't answer. By the next turn he was gasping for breath.

"Think you can make it?" Maureen called out. "We can alternate walking and running." She didn't want to insult him by stopping altogether. Boys had fragile egos, she knew, and she didn't want Jake to think she thought he was a wimp. He was just a little out of shape, that's all.

"I've got to quit, Maureen. All these dumb flowers are making me wheeze."

Jake veered off the path and flopped down on the grass. Every time he inhaled or exhaled she heard a high whistling sound. Max stood faithfully beside him.

"We better keep walking. It's dangerous to stop running suddenly. Are you OK, Jake?"

"I would be if I had my stupid inhaler," Jake replied curtly. Maureen knelt beside him and saw that he was having trouble breathing. "Would you believe when I came over here I locked myself out of the house? Now I can't get my asthma medication," he continued in between wheezes.

"Is it serious?"

"Not usually. But if I don't feel a lot better in a few minutes, I'm going to have to call my mother. She's at a meeting for the hospital auxiliary, her committee is—" Jake bent over, wracked by a fit of coughing.

Maureen grew alarmed. She knelt down beside him. "Jake, are you OK?" she cried.

"Don't worry. I'll be fine. I just need my medicine. Listen, can you run to a pay phone and call my mom at the hospital? My dad's out of town, so I can't reach him. I'm sure the staff can find Mom somewhere, though."

"You should have told me you had asthma. I didn't want to make you sick."

"I'm not sick," Jake said, his voice hoarse, his face tense. "And it's not your fault." But the way he said it made Maureen think that he did feel it was her fault. "If I know I'm going to be exercising a lot, like in gym, I take some medicine ahead of time, if I think of it. But I don't always need it. In fact, usually, I don't. That's why I don't bother to take my inhaler with me all the time anymore. It's been ages since I needed it."

He paused to catch his breath. "It's all the pollen in the air from these trees that did me in. Don't worry, I know what I have to do. Now, here's the number at the hospital. . . ."

But Maureen did worry. Jake gave her some change for the call, and she ran as fast as she could back over to the shopping area where she found a pay phone. But when she returned to where Jake was sitting, she noticed that he didn't sound—or look—any better. Even worse, a small crowd of other runners had gathered around Jake. The people were just concerned, but Jake apparently didn't enjoy being the center of attention. He was wheezing so hard he could barely speak, but he kept waving them away with his free hand—the other held Max's leash—and the expression on his face was grim. Even worse, he refused to talk to Maureen as they waited together for his mother. She knew he was having difficulty speaking, but he could have at least smiled at her occasionally, or let her know that he didn't think he was going to die.

But no matter what Maureen said or did, Jake refused to stop frowning. He told her in between wheezes to go home, but she refused to budge. When his mother arrived fifteen minutes later, she gave Maureen a frazzled smile and quickly helped Jake into the car. Max bounded into the backseat after him, and they drove off. Jake didn't even wave good-bye to her through the window.

As Maureen turned to go home herself, an older man stopped her. She recognized him as one of the runners who'd been circling the reservoir. "Hey, is there anything I can do?" he asked. "Is your boyfriend going to be OK?"

But all Maureen could do was shrug helplessly. Sudden tears blurred her vision, and she turned abruptly and began to run home. She certainly didn't know if Jake was going to be

OK. But she did know one thing: If there had been any chance of Jake's becoming her boyfriend before, there wasn't one any longer. After what happened that afternoon, she knew she'd lost Jake for good.

Eight

By the time she reached her house, Maureen was weak from hunger and totally exhausted. Mrs. Meyer saw her coming up the front path and rushed to the door.

"Maureen, you should've called! I've been so worried. You've been gone for hours. You couldn't have been running for all this time! What's happened?"

"Oh, Mom, it was awful." Her voice trembled as her mother put an arm around her and helped her inside. "Jake's sick—he collapsed with this awful asthma, and it's all my fault."

"Oh, no! Is he all right?"

"Yeah, at least I think he is—if he got to his medicine in time."

Maureen sank down in a kitchen chair and proceeded to tell her mother the whole story. As she spoke, Mrs. Meyer poured a glass of milk for her and began heating up a can of soup.

"Honey, you're being too hard on yourself,"

she finally said as she placed the hot soup and a plate of crackers in front of Maureen.

But Maureen would not be comforted. "No, I'm not, Mom," she cried, close to tears. "If only I hadn't talked him into running with me. He didn't want to, but I kept pushing him. I guess I embarrassed him into it. It wasn't fair to use those tactics."

"Maureen, dear—"

"Mom, I didn't know it would be dangerous for him. He never said anything about it. How could I have known?"

She put her head down on her arms and began to cry. All the tension of the last few hours was released, and her tears flowed freely.

Mrs. Meyer tried to comfort her. "You couldn't have known, sweetheart, but I can see how badly you feel. Now try not to worry. Here's your soup. You'll feel better after you eat something. And then you can call him and see how he is."

Maureen finished the soup, hardly tasting it, then headed upstairs for the phone.

Jake's line was busy for quite a while, but when she finally got through, it was his mother who answered—not Jake. He was fine now but resting, she was told. Mrs. Harmon promised to give her son the message, and she assured Maureen that she could talk to him the next day.

She had no better luck calling Jake at home the next day. She left numerous messages with whoever answered and a few more on the answering machine, but eventually she got the impression that she was becoming a nuisance. Mrs. Harmon was always excruciatingly polite, though, as she made excuses for Jake's not calling back.

It was such an ordeal—getting up the courage and forcing herself to call, but never talking to him. She longed to hear his voice, to hear him say he forgave her. She began to suspect that his parents weren't giving him her messages. Could he possibly be too sick to come to the phone? He probably just didn't want to talk to her. He might be angry—or embarrassed. She had to hear again that he didn't blame her. Although Jake hadn't gone to school that day, Mrs. Harmon had said she thought he'd be back the next day.

Tomorrow, thought Maureen. *We'll straighten things out tomorrow.*

But Maureen did not talk to Jake the next day in school, either. He was back, but somehow he never found the time to stop and chat with her in the halls. Maureen was devastated.

"He's avoiding me," Maureen told Debbie dejectedly. "I guess it's not going to work for us. Maybe it's for the best—we're just not interested in the same things. He's into photography, and I'm a runner. We don't have much in common."

"But there are lots of other things you could do together," Debbie urged, "like go to movies, have picnics . . . Look, I don't run, and we're still best friends."

Maureen's response was glum silence. Debbie sighed. "Any two people have *some* different interests," she went on.

"But running is my *main* interest. Does that mean I can never have a boyfriend?"

"Of course not. But, if you insist on a boy-friend who runs, you're going about it the wrong way. What you should do is hang around the track after school. You've been showing off those legs to the wrong crowd. If you want an athlete, go where the athletes are. Really, Mo, you've got to learn the basics."

"I don't know, Debbie."

"Remember last year when I wanted Steve to ask me to the Spring Thing? I knew he was going to be rehearsing for *The Diary of Anne Frank* almost every afternoon, so I volunteered to paint scenery. You've got to be where the action is! Not only was it fun, but I was right there during rehearsal breaks and was included in all the cast parties and everything."

"Smart move."

"So after a while my great charm and beauty were noticed, and I had a date to the dance."

"I thought you just liked painting sets."

"Of course I liked it, but having Steve around made it a lot more fun."

"I don't think I can do that. It's too hard. I don't want to chase boys. I'd rather let them find me."

"Me, too. But it doesn't work that way. Look, you've been waiting almost two years, and nobody's discovered you yet, even if you do have beautiful blond hair and big blue eyes. Anyway, it's not boy chasing. It's being assertive. What happened to all that stuff you learned in your support group last year? It'll work with boys just as it does with anyone else. If you like someone, don't just sit around waiting for the phone to ring, let him know you're interested—go places where he goes, talk to him. If you want to have dates, you're going to have to hustle. Believe me, this is the Voice of Experience talking."

Maureen couldn't understand why Jake didn't want to see her anymore, though. She knew she was attractive. People were always assuming she was popular and had lots of boyfriends—people who didn't know how she spent her Saturday nights, that is. Maybe it was her personality. It must mean she had a terrible personality. That had to be it.

She was starting to lose confidence in herself. When Jake had come over to her house last Friday, it had seemed perfectly natural that

115

he would want to spend time with her. But now she was beginning to have doubts. Maybe her comments hadn't been as amusing as she'd thought. He probably was really friendly like that with everyone—that's why he was so popular. Now that he knew what a one-track mind she had, he didn't want to have anything more to do with her.

It would be hard to forget him, but she decided to give Debbie's method a try. That day after taking her books home, Maureen headed back to school and the track. It was a hot dusty afternoon, and she wished she were out running along the river, or on the winding, shaded path along Fresh Pond. Anywhere but there. She sat down on the dry grass and started her warm-ups, wishing she could see water and sky instead of a brick wall.

"This had better be worth it," she mumbled. It was a quarter mile track. Twenty times around to go five miles. *Here goes the most boring half hour of my life,* she thought. Going around in a circle took the fun out of running. You never went anywhere. Never made any progress. She had to keep her fingers bent a certain way to count the laps, which made her feel ridiculous.

There were only a few other kids working out on the track. A couple of girls were practicing handing off a baton for relay runs, and two boys were doing hurdles. Not exactly a crowd of handsome suitors. Debbie might have the right idea, but this was definitely the wrong place.

Then she saw a familiar figure come out of the gym. Her heart skipped. It was Jake! He was standing in the shadow by the door changing lenses on that fancy camera of his. Maureen was at the far end of the track now and could barely see him. She wondered if he recognized her.

Then someone else came out—a girl!

Maureen rounded the bend and was running toward them. She was too far away to call out, not that she wanted to call attention to herself anyway, so she kept her eyes straight ahead as if she were totally absorbed in her activity while her mind raced in a different direction.

Out of the corner of her eye she could see that the girl also had a camera. *And* long dark hair—she was Oriental. All of a sudden Maureen remembered Mr. Devon's project. That must be the student Jake was supposed to tutor, the one from Japan. But not *after* school! He wasn't supposed to see her *after* school! She'd probably asked him for help with her camera. You'd think he could see through a trick like that.

Boy, everyone seemed to know this game better than she did. As she rounded the bend again, she saw them pick up their cameras and walk off toward the park. She heard laughter. Sounds as though Reiko knows pretty much English already, she thought. Enough to amuse Jake, anyway.

Maureen wished she hadn't followed Debbie's advice. She felt terrible. Not only had she ruined her run by staying on that tiny track, but she couldn't stop thinking about Jake and Reiko. For a minute she considered asking Jake to help her take pictures, too. But she couldn't. If he didn't want to talk to her, she wouldn't keep pestering him.

Anyway, she didn't care whether she took good pictures or not. If someone stuck a camera in her hands and smiled, she clicked the shutter. But that was it. She had absolutely no interest in doing more. Except for birthdays and vacations, her camera lay buried in a bottom drawer with a half-exposed roll of film in it waiting to be developed.

When Maureen reached the far end of the track again, she veered off through the gate and headed home. Enough of this torture, she thought. She ran around the neighborhood for a while planning how she was going to tell Debbie off for giving her such lousy advice.

As she ran past Debbie's house, she spotted her friend in the garage, sitting on a stack of old newspapers in front of her upside-down ten-speed. Debbie was trying to get the chain back on its sprockets. Maureen ran up the drive.

"Hi, Mo." She smiled as Maureen burst in

and flopped back against a stepladder. "Know anything about bikes? My chain fell off, and I can't seem to get it back on right. I knew this would happen sometime. I had to walk the dumb thing all the way home from the dentist's."

"No, Deb, I don't, and furthermore, I wish you hadn't told me to run at the school track. That was the worst idea you've ever had."

"Geez, I didn't think it was so bad. Wasn't anybody there? You can always try it another time, you know."

"Somebody was there, all right. Jake. Jake *and* Reiko, his ESL student."

"That is bad news."

"They looked as if they were going off to take pictures together. Debbie, it was awful. I had to go right past them before I could get off the track. I don't know if he saw me or not." Debbie was silent for a moment. Then she looked up at Maureen.

"Well, now you know where you stand, anyway," she said bluntly. "Maybe Jake isn't the right one for you. So my advice is still good. Give it another try."

"Debbie, I'm hooked on Jake. I don't want to date anyone else. I'd rather not have any dates. Even if I found another boy who liked to run, he probably couldn't take it if I ran faster. I'd always have to be worrying about showing him up, and that would be a big pain."

"Don't take it so hard," Debbie cajoled. "Things'll work out. Give it a little time. Maybe Jake will come to his senses."

No, Jake wasn't going to come to his senses, Maureen knew with sudden, sickening conviction. But *she* was. She wasn't angry with Debbie anymore, just herself. Debbie had only been trying to be helpful. Maureen was the real birdbrain—knocking herself out trying to get one of the best-looking, most popular boys in the junior class to notice *her*. It was a lost cause. She wasn't pretty enough or interesting enough or smart enough to have a boyfriend like that. Just because she'd had a little success at some dumb party, she'd lost all perspective and thought she had what it took to get the boy of her dreams. Ha! Wow, had she been foolish. Jake and Reiko were probably laughing at her right then.

Maureen wanted to run. She wanted to run and run and never stop—run away from that crummy school and those dumb kids and her big empty house and forget about everything.

Nine

Maureen tossed and turned all night with dreams of running—running after someone, running away, being chased herself. It was quite early when she woke up for good. But she knew there wasn't a chance she could still go back to sleep. She watched her room turn from black to soft gray as morning approached and felt as if she had come to a turning point. People, parties, the romance game—those weren't things she could ever really count on. Eventually she was bound to be disappointed. Chasing after boys—it was all so frivolous and wasteful. She'd wasted enough of her time already.

As it gradually got light enough to see, Maureen couldn't stand lying in bed any longer. She had to do something—make some change that would reflect her new attitude. Rising from her bed, she groped for a pair of scissors in the clutter of things on her dresser.

The blond curls fell in huge hunks as she

grabbed handful after handful, sawing away with the dull scissors. All the anger of the past week came out. She was mad at Jake for being so proud and stubborn, and at Debbie for being popular, and at herself for falling in love with someone who wouldn't love her back—mad at her hair which reminded her of how far short of everyone's expectations she had fallen. When her hair, which had been a symbol of her vanity, was gone, she'd be ready for a fresh start. No longer would she be tempted to play a romance game she couldn't ever win.

In a few minutes it was over. She looked down and saw five years' growth of hair in piles at her feet. With every cut, a worry had disappeared; her mind was clear at last. Now she wanted to run.

Her running clothes were still damp from the previous afternoon, but she put them on anyway, anxious to get outside as fast as possible. Tossing an old sweatshirt over them against the cool morning air, she burst out into the deserted street.

She loped along slowly for a while to warm up her muscles and shake out the stiffness, then she stretched her legs and sprinted easily for a mile or so. It would be a good day, she thought—not too hot, not too cold. A day like that could take her mind off anything. Even a broken heart.

Maureen never minded running by herself.

Although it was nice running with her dad, and of course she would have loved running with Jake, being by herself was also satisfying. She always felt wonderfully independent. In all the miles she'd run, no one had ever bothered her. It never seemed as if she was running through a big city, but as if she were isolated in a capsule in her own time and space—in the world, yet apart.

The streets were quiet and empty. Only a few buses and delivery trucks had started their morning runs. She ignored the traffic lights and crossed the side streets after a quick glance up and down without breaking stride.

A loud, harsh bark and throaty growl interrupted the early-morning bird sounds. A big, black dog with a thick, ugly face was pressing up against a wooden gate barking threateningly. Suddenly the latch gave way, and he bounded out into the street, barking and snapping at her heels.

Quickly she crossed over to the far side, hoping to get out of his territory before things got nasty, but he seemed to claim the whole length of the street.

"Down, boy. Down!" she shouted, glancing around as she ran, hoping to find a stick or something to ward him off with. Runners and mailmen always had the same problem when it came to dogs. As she passed a row of trash cans lined up on the curb ready for early pickup, she grabbed the handle of a discarded broom and waved the worn bristle end back toward the dog's face.

"Down. Get down!" she commanded again.

He pulled back, snarling and watching as Maureen raced ahead, clutching her weapon tightly in one hand. She would keep it handy, just in case.

Up ahead she spotted a fellow jogger, a balding, heavyset man, who panted loudly as he hauled his excess bulk up a slight hill. He was listening to his Walkman and didn't hear Maureen close behind him.

When suddenly he caught sight of her and her yellow broom out of the corner of his eye, he jumped, stumbling and falling as he lost his concentration.

"You look as if you'd seen a ghost," Maureen said as she paused to help him to his feet.

"You mean *witch*, don't you? You scared the daylights out of me, sneaking up behind me like that with that broom. You should give us ordinary people a little warning, you know," he said, as he brushed the dirt off a bruised knee.

"Sorry, didn't mean to startle you, but you don't have to shout. I can hear fine."

He reached up and pulled his earphones down around his neck. "I guess it wasn't your fault. My Walkman was on a little too loud. Do you always run this early? I'm not used to having company at this hour."

They ran along together for a while chatting about morning runs, the weather, and dog problems before Maureen, tiring of his slower pace, waved good-bye and headed off on her own.

As she pulled ahead, she noticed how different it felt to have short hair. Her head felt so light—no wispy strands blowing across her face or banner of curls billowing out behind her. Her ears felt chilly and unprotected. Then a terrible thought occurred to her. That man had practically called her a witch . . . because of the broom of course, but could it be . . . What did her hair look like?

She headed home.

Taking the stairs two at a time, she ran up to her room to take a closer look at what she'd done. She stopped short as she confronted the unfamiliar face in the mirror and the hair hanging half out of the wastebasket next to the dresser. She stared silently into the mirror, aghast at what that burst of predawn fury had accomplished.

Why had she acted so impulsively? Usually she mulled things over in her mind for days, even weeks, before taking action, but not this time. She wished with all her heart that she hadn't done it. She grabbed the hand mirror and surveyed the damage from every angle.

Twenty different lengths, curls sticking out in all directions. It looked as if she'd been playing "beauty shop" with a three-year-old.

Her good mood from the morning was fading fast. She sat for a few minutes in a daze, wondering what to do next. A soft knock on the door roused her.

"Maureen, it's almost time for school." It was her mother.

She didn't answer.

"Maureen, are you all right?" The door opened a crack, and Mrs. Meyer stuck her head in. "May I come in?

"What have you *done*?" she cried out, knowing the answer as soon as she spoke. Quickly she walked over and stood behind her daughter. "What happened, honey?" she asked softly as she saw Maureen's hopeless expression. "This is going to take some getting used to. You know, I think I was more attached to those curls than you were," she said as she put her hands on Maureen's shoulders.

"Mom, I don't want to be pretty anymore. And I don't want to worry about boyfriends. I just want to run."

"I know it can be hard when you don't look the way you feel. When I was young, I was tall for my age. People always expected me to act more grown-up. My cousin, Cathy, used to get away with murder because she was so little and cute and innocent-looking. But I was expected to 'know better.' "

"Everyone expects me to be Miss Popularity."

"Even though some people judge you by your looks, you'll just have to try to be yourself."

"I will be. I'm through with all this socializing and big-girl stuff. From now on, I'm going to devote myself to more serious, worthwhile things. I'm through with being pretty."

"I'm sorry, honey, but I think you'll always look pretty. No matter what goofy hairstyle you try, you'll always have the prettiest face in the world. At least, in my opinion."

"Mom"—Maureen turned to her mother, her eyes pleading—"what am I going to do? I can't go to school like this."

"I'm afraid you wouldn't blend into the crowd at this point, and it's going to take a lot more than twenty minutes to make you presentable."

"Is there any hope?" Maureen asked.

"Of course. I guess you can stay home this morning, and we'll see if Larry can fix you up. We'll tell him it's an emergency."

As she leaned back in the huge leather chair and stared at her reflection in the oversize mirror, a small face above a shapeless tent of plastic, Maureen started to relax. She was in the hands of an expert. Larry never made mistakes. He always knew what to do. She settled into his chair with complete faith in his ability to repair the results of her fit of temper.

Larry wasn't the kind of person you expected to find cutting hair. He was big. He looked as if he could have played football, maybe. But he *was* handy with a pair of scissors. And most important of all, he was interested in your opinion.

Some people in beauty shops just started cutting, especially if you were young. They knew what they wanted to do, and that's the kind of cut you got. But not Larry. He spent a lot of time discussing your hair, how you thought it should look, and what was practical, so you always knew what was going on.

"You've really given me a challenge here, kid," Larry teased as he leaned against the wall surveying the damage. "Guess this 'punk' look isn't right for you after all, is it?"

She let him think she'd done it on purpose. "No, I'm not sure what style I want now."

They discussed the possibilities for a while, then Larry went to work. Maureen closed her eyes and let her head fill with the blaring rock music, which made conversation unnecessary. It was just as well, she didn't feel like talking.

An hour later Maureen looked one hundred percent better. Her mother seemed relieved when she walked in the door. It was important to her that everything look nice, daughters included.

Maureen was glad Larry was able to fix her up. She didn't really want to look ugly, but she was still determined to put boys and dates out of her mind and concentrate on training for a race, maybe even the marathon. She couldn't wait to talk to her father about the best way to train.

Armed with a note from her mother saying she was late because of a morning "appointment," Maureen was back in school by the end of third period. She headed to the library to wait for Trang.

She spent a few minutes arranging the notes for her lesson while the classes changed. As the noises in the hall died down, she looked up and saw Trang walking in, a big grin on her face.

"Hi, Trang. You look happy today."

Trang kept smiling. "You very short," Trang said.

"Who, me? I'm not short. I'm almost five-eight."

"No, you hair!"

"Oh, yeah, I almost forgot. Guess I look a lot different. You like it?"

"You very pretty. I like," Trang added as she sat down, still smiling.

I guess you have to do something pretty dramatic to get a response, Maureen thought. This was the first spontaneous conversation she and Trang had had. She tried to keep it going.

"Do you like short hair?"

"Yes, I like."

"You can get a haircut, too!"

"I like, but . . . I . . . uh . . . No curl. Maybe no pretty like you."

"No, you try it, Trang. You'll be pretty, you'll see." Since Trang was short herself, Maureen felt that the younger girl would look good with a neat, short haircut, but it was very difficult to convince Trang of that. After a few minutes of trying, Maureen decided to go on to the lesson she'd planned.

Hoping to avoid questions about her hair and her morning absence, Maureen went straight to the trolley station after school. She could deal with everyone's curiosity better on Monday when she herself was more used to the way she looked.

Debbie would sure be surprised. And Jake . . . Well, it didn't really matter, did it? She wouldn't be seeing much of him.

Mr. Devon had announced a tutor's meeting for next week, and she was feeling nervous about the upcoming session. Jake would be there. They hadn't spoken once since that terrible day at the reservoir. On one hand, she wanted desperately to see him, but on the other, she dreaded the confrontation.

What would she say? She hoped she could think of something appropriate. If only she knew how he would react. Would he be hostile? Friendly? Or ignore her altogether? That would be the worst. She could stand anything but that.

The opposite of love is not hate but indifference. She remembered somebody telling her that once and suddenly realized it was true. Maybe Jake wasn't going to fall in love with her, but he had to *care* about her, just a little. Didn't he? Only by confronting him face to face in the tutoring session would she be able to find out where she stood. But what if she didn't like what she found out?

Ten

The dreaded staff meeting turned out to be mainly a picnic-planning meeting. Mr. Devon wanted the foreign students and their tutors to get together for a big end-of-the-year party, and he wanted to have it on Friday so it wouldn't conflict with all the class parties and dances in June.

All Maureen could remember about the planning session was that she had volunteered to bring cupcakes. Her mind had been in a turmoil for most of the meeting, waiting for Jake to arrive. She had *tried* to pay attention by focusing her eyes on Mr. Devon's desk and forcing herself not to look at the door every two minutes to see if he was there. When she finally heard someone come in, she couldn't help turning, but it was only Mike, sheepishly slipping into a back-row seat. Jake was conspicuously absent, and the dreaded confrontation was temporarily put off.

                              *   *   *

Until Friday, that is: the day of the picnic
dinner. Maureen was again faced with the di-
lemma of what to wear. She desperately flung
one rejected outfit after another onto her bed as
she tried to pick out something smashing. The
pile was mounting.

Her new white jeans? No, she was bound to
get grass stains on them. Tan shorts? Pink
overalls? At last she settled on a pair of blue
cotton slacks with a striped T-shirt and oversize white jacket with the sleeves rolled up. The
outfit would be comfortable, *and* it looked good.

She wondered if it was sensible to spend so
much time on her appearance when she had
recently vowed to stop thinking about Jake—
and boys in general. It *was* sort of contradic-
tory. But as her mother said, "You should look
nice to please yourself and not worry about everyone else."

Still, she wondered if Jake would notice her
haircut. Of course he'd notice; but what would
he think? Debbie thought it made her look glamorous, but she still wasn't quite sure.

Well, off to the picnic. It started at five o'clock
and was being held at Andersen Park, the perfect place for a large picnic. There was a roofed-
over area with several grills ringed by picnic
tables, which had been reserved for the group.
A small pond curved around the grassy hills,

and a couple of baseball diamonds flanked the picnic area.

She stopped in the kitchen to pick up the cupcakes she had baked and placed them carefully on the backseat of the car.

"Have a good time, honey," her mother said as she dropped her off at the park. "Call if you need a ride home."

Maureen had started out the day excited, determined to enjoy herself, but now as she gazed at all the unfamiliar faces she began to have second thoughts.

She hardly knew a soul. Of the three people she did know, she couldn't talk to Jake, she hadn't been too friendly with Mike lately, and Trang hardly talked at all. That might make for a pretty dull evening. Too bad Debbie wouldn't be there to give her some moral support.

She walked slowly over to the group and placed her cupcakes on the dessert table.

Then panic set in. Her hands grew cold and sweaty. She couldn't focus her thoughts on anything. It was like the way she used to feel when she was a little girl before her ballet recitals, ready to throw up at the slightest provocation. Her dance teacher had always said, "When you're scared to death, smile."

So that's what Maureen did. She gave everyone the biggest, friendliest smile she could summon, accompanied by an enthusiastic hello.

They seemed to be falling for it. Everyone smiled back.

Everyone but Jake. He was standing by the hot dog and hamburger table sipping a Coke. Dressed in a navy polo shirt and khaki pants, his face flushed from the afternoon's activities, Jake looked incredibly attractive. Maureen had an overwhelming desire to rush over and hug him. Her dear, sweet, funny Jake—how could things not be right between them. Maureen started over to him.

"Hi, Jake." She was still smiling halfheartedly. "It's nice to see you again—it's been awhile. Are you feeling OK?"

But Jake's mouth was tense as he answered. "Hi, Maureen. Sure, I'm OK. I guess people who try to show off deserve to get in trouble." He laughed nervously.

"I'm really sorry, Jake. I didn't mean to push you into anything you couldn't handle. I just . . ."

"Yeah, I know. You couldn't have known I was such a wimp. It wasn't your fault."

"But, Jake, you're not . . ."

"Maureen, I really don't want to talk about it. Forget it, OK?"

"OK." Maureen swallowed, fighting to keep her emotions under control. This sarcastic person didn't sound like the Jake she loved. What had made him change this way?

They both glanced around, trying to find a way to escape this conversation. Before either of them could locate another group to talk to, Mr. Devon joined them.

"Glad you kids could come. We're going to have a great picnic. Just look at the sky. Not a cloud in sight. You know," he continued, "you've both done a terrific job so far. I think your students are really making progress. Trang, especially, is doing well."

"Oh? You really think so?" Maureen started to brighten up a bit. "I was afraid I wasn't doing much good. She's always so quiet. I'm never sure how much I've taught her."

"Well, don't get discouraged. It takes a long time to learn a new language, especially when you're shy. So please don't give up. You're doing fine. How about you, Jake? Having any problems?"

"No. Reiko is a good student. I think she studies *too* hard. If we all studied English as much as she does, you'd have a classful of straight-A students."

"It would be nice if you all started taking after her instead of vice versa." Mr. Devon laughed. "I see you brought your camera. Will our picnic be immortalized in the yearbook?"

"Sure. Reiko wanted some help with her new camera, so I'm giving her some pointers."

Mr. Devon turned to Maureen. "Are you a photographer, too?"

"Well, I try—when we go on vacation."

"We're going to get some nature shots with these close-up lenses," Jake hurried on. "Reiko found some interesting mushrooms on a stump back in the woods. We're going to take a series of shots under different lighting conditions while the sun goes down. What kind of camera do you have, Maureen?"

"Well, uh, I use one of those disc cameras."

"Oh, I guess you'll have to stick to snapshots, then. You can't do much with a camera like that," Jake told her, sounding very professional.

"Maybe not. I'm not really interested in mushrooms, anyway," Maureen retorted, and turning abruptly, she walked away.

Her determination to have a good time was gone. Jake really had a chip on his shoulder. He said he didn't blame her, but it sure sounded as if he were mad at someone. She flopped down under a tree and rested her head on her bent knees.

Since she couldn't find anyone to talk to, Maureen decided to help get the fire started. She noticed Trang also sitting by herself a little forlornly and decided to volunteer them both as cooks. She pulled herself up, tried to smile, and headed over to Trang.

"Hi, Trang. Want to help get the charcoal started? Come on. It's over here."

They hauled a twenty-five-pound bag over and poured some into each grate—one for hot dogs and one for hamburgers—then went to look for Mr. Devon to get matches. They lit the fires, then sat quietly, fanning the coals as the kids started to line up around the tables.

"You hungry, Trang?" Maureen asked as she opened the bags of buns.

"Yes, I like chip." Maureen laughed and glanced over at her friend affectionately.

"You're well on your way to becoming an American if you've already developed a craving for potato chips. The trouble with being a cook, though, is the rest of the food will be gone before we get a chance at it. Here, put these hamburgers on the grill while I go get us some chips."

Maureen returned with one plateful of chips and one of carrots, so she and Trang had something to munch on as they grilled the food.

"That's better. Now we're all set."

It was hot work, but Maureen enjoyed her stint at the grill. She wasn't obligated to talk to anyone; and yet everyone, when they came up to get served, took the time to chat with her a little.

You've found the perfect solution to your troubles, she told herself. *Become a short-order cook!* Finally everyone was served, and Maureen and Trang helped themselves to the two remaining burgers.

She felt closer to Trang now. Sharing a job

with her let Maureen get to know her better, even if they didn't talk much. Trang looked as if she were a pretty handy cook even with something as American as hamburgers.

"Where'd you learn to cook, Trang? Do you make hamburgers at home?"

Trang looked up. "No hamburger. Rice and vegetable only. Maybe chicken or little fish. My brother, sometime he catch fish."

"I bet you have to help out a lot."

"Yes, I help mother. She teach me Vietnam cooking."

"Could you teach me sometime? I'd like to learn how to make spring rolls. We get them at a take-out place near our home. They're great. I wish I could make them for my dad. He loves them."

"Maybe I ask my mother it's OK."

"That would be great. Thanks, Trang. I'd really like that."

After dinner someone made a campfire. Maureen was glad to see that kids were sitting in small groups of three and four, not paired off as they did at most school events.

Mike had brought his guitar, and so as they sat around the campfire roasting marshmallows they sang old favorites. Mr. Devon passed out the words to some of the songs so that everyone could join in. As it got too dark to read, one of the students taught the group a

Mexican folk song. Then someone else taught everybody an Israeli song, and Maureen pulled Trang up to join in a circle dance around the fire. It was finally dark, and the picnic began to break up. After helping to clean up, Maureen looked around to see if she could get a ride home with anyone, but all the cars seemed full. She wished she had asked her mom to pick her up, because the pay phone was broken.

"Maureen. You need a ride?"

It was Jake—followed by Reiko, of course.

"I think we can squeeze you in . . . if you don't mind the backseat," he added.

"Backseat" was an understatement. Jake had a beat-up old MG with room for a three-year-old child behind the bucket seats. It would be humiliating to tag along, but she had no choice. Hardly anyone else was left in the parking lot.

"Hop in," Jake invited. "We'll stow our cameras and stuff on the floor up here."

He seemed to be in a better mood. Either Reiko or those dumb mushrooms must have cheered him up. She decided not to hold their earlier conversation against him and to relax and enjoy the ride. She did love convertibles, and no one else she knew had one. As she felt the night air whip against her cheeks, she missed her long hair. What could be more irresistible than long blond hair streaming out from a bright blue convertible? Driving along, Maureen couldn't help fantasizing that she was the one beside Jake in the front seat instead of crouched in back, knees up to her chin, unpleasantly close to a defective muffler. All at once, the ride was ruined for her, and she closed her eyes, grateful that she didn't have to say anything now.

They dropped Reiko off first. Maureen climbed into the front seat, anxious to stretch out her long legs but still grateful for the noisy muffler. As they pulled into her driveway, Jake turned off the motor and put his hand on hers. Maureen's heart started to pound.

"Maureen, I'm sorry." He squeezed her hand. "I'm really not mad at you for what happened. I'm mad at myself. I wish I could do the things you like to do. I wanted to so much, and I thought I could if I tried hard enough. That was pretty dumb, and I made a fool of myself. I enjoy sports, but I'm not in your league, and I only want to do something if I can do it really well. I guess I admired you because you could do something I couldn't. You made it look so easy, I thought for a minute that I could be part of it with you."

Jake's arm moved around to her shoulder, and she felt his fingers lightly touch her neck. She shivered in spite of the warm night.

"Why did you cut your hair?" he whispered

as he fingered the remaining short curls brushing her ears.

"Well, it's sort of hard to explain." She hesitated. "I guess I just felt like a change." She still couldn't discuss the feelings that had swamped her usual rational approach to things.

"I'll miss seeing those gorgeous curls."

She felt an ache in her throat as his fingers brushed through her hair, and a warmth of feeling spread through her body as his hand came to rest on her shoulder.

Oh, Jake, I wouldn't have cut my hair if it weren't for you, Maureen thought. There were so many different feelings and emotions coursing through her that she felt both excited and confused. What was he trying to say to her? How did he feel? But in the next instant, her hopes came crashing down.

"I can see it wouldn't work for us, Maureen. You know it wouldn't," Jake said as he pulled back his arm and she dropped back against the seat.

"What do you mean?" Her voice wavered.

"I can't share the thing you care about most. You have your goals, you're a runner. And I have mine. And they're very different. It's better that we've discovered that now, before we're too emotionally involved." He held her chin and looked into her eyes.

"But I'm already emotionally involved. Very.

143

Please, please stop talking like this. I don't care if you don't run. It doesn't matter."

"After a while it would matter. It would come between us," he answered firmly.

Right then, Maureen didn't care about running or anything else in the world. All she wanted was to feel his arms around her.

But Jake hopped out of the car. *No! Stop!* Maureen cried silently. She didn't want to get out, didn't want him to leave. He walked around to open her door, then took her by the hand. They walked arm in arm to her front door, which was darkened by the shadows of an old oak tree.

"Mo, we'll still be friends. If you want to, we could work together on the tutoring project again. That afternoon was fun. I just wanted to straighten things out between us. I'm sorry I never called you back when I started feeling better. I was going to, a hundred times, but I couldn't. I was too angry with myself, and too embarrassed. I'm not very good at explaining my feelings. I just knew right then that I couldn't be the kind of person you were looking for."

She could feel the tears welling up behind her eyes. If she said another word, she'd start to cry. Pulling her hand from his, Maureen turned and ran into the house, almost stumbling on the steps in the dark.

Once inside, she went straight upstairs and crawled into bed without even turning on the light. She hated to see herself in the mirror when she was crying.

Eleven

The next morning, a sunny Saturday, Maureen slept late. She was still running a brush through her hair when she heard the doorbell ring, then rapid footsteps on the stairs.

"Mo, I'm dying! Tell me quick! What happened at the picnic?" Debbie was breathless from running upstairs. She sat down on the bed, her legs tucked under her.

"Well, now I know why Jake didn't return my calls."

"You do? It was his parents, wasn't it? They thought the whole thing was your fault, so they didn't give him your messages, did they?"

"Nope, he got the messages, all right. But he decided that since he couldn't run, he wasn't the right person for me. Since he didn't want to start a relationship, he didn't call back. I guess he was embarrassed, too."

"That creep, he could at least have called! Didn't he know how rotten you felt? And he ought to let *you* decide what kind of boyfriend you want."

"Yeah. The worst part is, he likes me."

"Well, that's *something*!"

"But he just wants to be 'friends.' "

"Oh, no! I hate when boys say that when they break up with you. How can you stand it?"

"I can't," Maureen admitted. She looked at Debbie sorrowfully. "I'm miserable. It wouldn't be so bad if he were mad at me or hated me. I could probably get over it. But how can I be friends with someone who makes me shiver every time he looks in my eyes . . . and makes my heart jump every time we touch? He wants to work on our tutoring projects together again, but I don't think I could handle it. I just couldn't act normally."

"You could try. Maybe he'll change his mind. If you *really don't* care about whether he runs or not, maybe he'll finally believe you and change his mind. He's nuts if he doesn't."

"I don't want to throw myself at him," Maureen declared angrily. "He said he doesn't want to start a relationship, and that's that. It's his decision. And maybe it's for the best. Now I won't have to worry about dividing my time between Jake and running. Running is all I have left. And I'm going to give it all I've got."

"Hold on, Maureen. You're giving up too easily," Debbie argued. "If you go off and do nothing but run, you'll be proving him right. Why do you have to be so single-minded? And what about the old saying, opposites attract? That could be you and Jake. You really could date him and be a runner, both, but you're the one who seems to be making it impossible now." She paused, but Maureen said nothing. "Think it over, OK? I've got to go now. My mom is taking me shopping this morning. Talk to you later, if you're still around."

"Yeah, I'll be here. My dad's out of town this weekend."

Maureen spent the whole morning lying on her bed thinking about her predicament. No matter how she looked at it—lying on her back with her feet propped against the wall, flat on her stomach with her head buried in her arms, or lounging against the pillows and staring out into the clusters of spring leaves and newly opened buds just outside her window—she came to the same conclusion. She was drawn to Jake more than anyone she'd ever met.

"I love you." Whispering those three little words to herself made her wish with all her heart that she could be hearing them instead of saying them. But, no—Jake was right. He knew her better than she knew herself. What she really loved was the feeling she got when she pushed herself an extra mile or cut thirty seconds off her time. Testing herself, proving herself—she could *never* give that up! She had been right to decide to give up boys. Running was ultimately more satisfying.

Romance and running didn't mix. She and Jake were like oil and water. You could put them together, but sooner or later they were driven apart.

Jake understood it, and so must she. She'd just have to be miserable until she could forget him.

When Debbie called that afternoon, Maureen's mind was made up. She answered on the hall phone and unwound the extra-long cord so she could sit in her room by the window and look at the sky as she talked.

"There's only one solution," she began. "I'm going to run in the marathon next spring. I'll start running two hours a day instead of one. My dad said you're supposed to run twice the length of the race you're training for every week. That's only fifty-two miles a week. I can do fifteen miles a day easily, which makes seventy-five miles a week if I only run five days a week. Then on the other two days I'll work out with weights and build up my leg muscles."

"Wow," Debbie said, sounding amused, "this sounds like higher mathematics to me. You really have everything figured out, don't you? Next you'll be making charts and graphs to keep track of your progress."

"Debbie, you're a genius. That's a terrific idea. I'll make a chart of my schedule with all my runs and average speeds and everything and put it all on a graph to show how fast I'm improving. Maybe I can get extra credit in gym for it."

"Mo, I was *kidding*," Debbie said, sounding a little more worried. "You're taking all this too seriously. You don't have to give up on humanity just because of Jake. How about Mike, from your English class? I bet he'd ask you out in a minute if you ever gave him any encouragement. Don't get so fanatical."

"Deborah," Maureen replied with great seriousness, "all runners are fanatical. It goes with the territory. You have to be, or you never get any better. That's what my dad says. You have to decide what's important and not let anything get in your way. He's really going to be proud of me when I finish the marathon next spring. I know he will."

"Sure he will, Mo. But what about me? Do you think you'll be able to squeeze some time for me into your schedule?"

"You? Well—what did you say your name was again?" Maureen teased. Debbie rolled her eyes in mock exasperation. "Yes, of course I'll still have time for you. But seriously, now, running's got to come first."

"Mmmm, at least we can talk at lunch. You can't give up eating."

"Hey, now that you mention it, I think I'll have to get my weight down a little. A few extra pounds can make a big difference, you know."

"I don't think you'll have much to worry about with all the exercise you're planning. Come on, Wonder Woman, it's time to use your brains for a change."

"OK, I'll be over in ten minutes."

Maureen hung up the phone, grabbed her books, and went over to Debbie's where they started doing their math homework. But after every problem, Maureen paused a minute or two to plan her training strategy. She had heard that the winner last year had trained on Heartbreak Hill. That must have been agonizing. It worked, though. He passed the leader of the race on the hill, and no one caught up to him after that. He knew what the worst part of the race would be like, and he knew he could do it. That's what she would do, too. On weekends she'd run Heartbreak Hill.

The first thing Maureen learned was that Heartbreak Hill wasn't just one big hill; it was a series of hills that came at just the point in the race where you wanted to collapse. She could barely make it up one; and on the second her calf muscles started to cramp up, and she had to walk for a while. These hills were a hundred times harder than flat ground. She had been doing too much of her running along the river lately. *I'll have to add some special exercises to my routine to stretch out those muscles,* she thought.

Maureen felt invigorated by the challenge she'd set for herself. If something was hard, she loved it all the more; and she needed to have a direction, a goal to pursue, to take her mind off Jake. For the next two weeks, running filled all her thoughts. She bought *Runners' World* at the newsstand and pored over every issue, looking for tips. In addition to doing the hill twice a week, she had started interval training—doing part of her run for speed. Slowly her overall speed improved, and she felt terrific.

It was wonderful . . . sometimes painful, sometimes lonely, but wonderful. She was pushing herself hard and getting closer to her goal.

There was no time now to think about Jake, except when she came across him walking around with his camera—usually alone, but sometimes with Reiko. Then she would feel a twinge and wish she were walking beside him, laughing and holding hands. Sometimes she waved a friendly hello as she ran past. Other times, if she felt her emotions coming to the surface, she just ran faster—till it hurt. Pain could push away feelings.

Her dad had been pretty understanding when she told him she couldn't spend as much time with him as she used to. Weekends were when she worked on the hill. He was just surprised that it was running rather than a boyfriend that was taking up so much of her time.

She managed to find time to still see Debbie, though. But even their friendship seemed a little strained. Except for the schoolwork that she had to do, Maureen had little interest in anything but running. *When they see me cross that finish line, they'll see that it was all worth it,* she thought.

The one person she was still as strongly committed to was Trang. They continued to work together every day, and Maureen was proud of her progress. She was looking forward to the cooking lesson at Trang's house and was fascinated to hear about Trang's life in Vietnam and about her family. Trang had not been born until after the Vietnam War, so she had no memories of American soldiers.

Maureen wondered what it would be like to be part of a large family such as Trang's or Karen Rider's. She tried to imagine herself in Karen Rider's shoes as the only girl with a bunch of brothers. It would be convenient in that she could study boys right in her own home—in their natural environment. That was probably why Karen could handle them so well.

Usually Maureen didn't mind being an only child: she didn't have to share her stuff; she never had to wear hand-me-down clothes; when the family went on long drives, she always got to sit by the window—either window. But sometimes she did feel as though she were missing out on some fun. There was no one to talk to at night and no one to tease.

She added a couple of miles to her run that afternoon, knowing she might have to shorten her time the next day when she went to Trang's.

Trang didn't live too far from Maureen and Debbie's neighborhood—just across Beacon Street in an area of older brick apartment buildings. They weren't kept up too well anymore, the outside trim was peeling, but the entrance halls were elegant—marble floors, mahogany paneling, and high ceilings.

On the afternoon of the cooking lesson Maureen arrived right on time, at three o'clock. Standing at the front entrance, she waited to be buzzed in, her hand resting on the doorknob. Trang's family lived on the fourth floor—quite a climb if they were carrying groceries. At the top Trang stood waiting.

"Please come in. I happy you come my house. Please, sit. My mother make tea."

The living room was large and bright and almost totally empty. A few mats and pillows lined the walls, and there were two straight-backed chairs where Trang indicated they should sit. Maureen would have been more comfortable on the pillows, but Trang seemed determined to use the chairs. She could hear children playing in one of the back rooms and women's voices in the kitchen, but she and Trang sat alone in the hot front room for about ten minutes until a tiny gray-haired lady dressed entirely in black came in carrying a tray with a beautiful silver teapot and two cups of tea.

Maureen's cup was burning hot. There was no handle, just a delicate porcelain bowl that she grasped as lightly as possible with two hands, hoping it would cool off quickly.

"My aunt," Trang whispered.

"Hello, I'm Maureen. Nice to meet you."

The woman smiled and bowed courteously before returning to the kitchen.

Maureen was anxious to get started. This was a little too formal for her. At last the tea was cool enough to drink, and she gulped it down.

"Come on. Let's start cooking," she said, encouraging Trang to move.

"OK. Come this way." Trang led her through a long, narrow hall to the kitchen in back, where a large table in the middle of the room was piled with ingredients. A pair of huge cleavers rested on a chopping block, and vegetables and packets of unusual seeds and powders lined one side of the table. "First we chop," Trang instructed.

Trang pushed one of the knives toward Maureen along with a large knobby brown ginger root, which was the first of many things they would chop that afternoon.

Two hours later Maureen, Trang, and her two younger sisters had four dozen neatly rolled and stuffed dough packets waiting beside the frying pan. It was obviously fun for Trang to change roles and be the teacher for once, and Maureen was quite impressed with her pupil's culinary skills.

She tried to write down everything they had done while the sisters took over the frying.

After sampling a few of the delicious rolls as they came out of the hot oil, they packed a box for Maureen to take home—some for her mother and herself for dinner and some for her dad.

When she finally got home, it was late. There was still enough time for a workout, but she'd have to hurry. She never skipped a day now. She knew she was supposed to take it easy one day a week, but she couldn't stand to miss that day.

She changed and did a few quick stretches before running out the door. The cooking had been interesting—not exactly fun, but interesting. But she did resent the time it had taken from her run. She vowed to push herself a little harder to make up for it.

Maureen started out at a pretty fast pace, even though her legs felt stiff and heavy from the hours of sitting at school and then standing in Trang's kitchen. When she postponed her workout till late in the day, it was always harder to get started. She wished she'd stretched out a little more.

Her mind was dragging along an unwilling body. She had to keep thinking about her legs to make them go. Finally, after a mile or two it got easier, and she started to relax. Heading down Beacon Street alongside the heavy rush-hour traffic and after-work joggers, she felt comfortable. She belonged to this city of runners now. She could run with the best of them. She'd show everyone at the marathon next spring—a few hills couldn't stop her. Maureen decided to cut over to Commonwealth Avenue and tackle those hills now. If she did Heartbreak Hill, she could eat a few more spring rolls without feeling guilty.

As Maureen approached the crest of the last hill, she remembered the day she and Debbie had watched the marathon. She remembered the runners' faces. Their concentration was total: eyes staring straight ahead, oblivious of everything but their own bodies; throbbing veins, blisters rubbed raw, the searing pain of muscles worked beyond endurance. Now she knew what it was like, knew what made them keep going. With a surge of pride, she thought, *I'm one of them.*

Then it happened. She felt something snap. A hot, sharp pain stabbed through her right knee and drove all other thoughts from her mind. Clutching her knee, Maureen sat down hard on the curb, her leg twisting uncomfortably beneath her, unable to take another step.

She sat there for a few minutes trying not to cry. She couldn't get up! And the usually busy street was now suddenly deserted. She'd have to get help.

There were houses all along the road, but most were set back from the street and had a lot of stairs. With a tremendous effort she struggled painfully to her feet and hopped along the sidewalk, wincing at each impact. Every time she came to a tree she stopped to rest till the throbbing subsided. But she kept going till she came to a house that sat on level ground. She made it up the walk, rang the bell, and leaned against the door, breathing hard and fighting back tears. Somebody *had* to be home. She couldn't take another step.

The woman who answered the door was sympathetic when Maureen in a confused rush of words explained what had happened.

"Oh, I know just how you feel, dear. I'm a jogger, too." Maureen couldn't help looking incredulous; the large woman looked like anything but a runner. "My girlfriend and I jog a mile every day after breakfast. Every day. Unless it's raining, of course. Last winter I slipped on some ice and twisted my ankle. I couldn't jog for a month. Well, actually, I was glad for the excuse. It was pretty cold that month. So I know how painful it can be. Come on in and sit down. Can I call a cab for you? Where do you live, dear?"

"Thanks, but I'd better call my mom first. If she's home, she can pick me up. I really appreciate your help."

"These hills around here are murder, aren't they?"

"Yeah, they're pretty hard if you're not used to them."

The woman chattered on while Maureen dialed. The initial relief of finding some help faded as the pain in her knee increased. In the back of her mind she knew it wasn't something that would go away in a day or two like a little pull or strain. She tried to keep smiling and nodding as the woman talked and she waited for her mom, but it was getting hard.

"Heartbreak Hill," what a perfect name for it! She sat in a wheelchair clutching an ice pack to her throbbing knee, waiting for the doctor in the emergency room to return with her X rays. Now it was her mother chattering away, trying to cheer her up, but it wasn't working. She'd put too much of herself into running to stop now. That's what the doctor was going to tell her to do, though. She knew it. He'd come in and give her that compassionate look before saying, "I'm sorry, Maureen." And then she'd know that it was all over.

After several more minutes of imagining the worst, Maureen was summoned by a nurse to go with her mother back into the doctor's office. The doctor was sitting on his desk looking at the X rays clipped to a light screen on the wall. Maureen held her breath.

"Well, it looks like nothing's broken, but I'm not sure yet what the problem is," he announced. "Have you been doing anything unusual?"

When she recounted her training schedule, the doctor began to nod. "I see. Well, that could be the problem right there. Let me see your feet. Shoes off. Mmm-hmm. Morton's foot."

"What?"

"Morton's foot. Look at your toes. See? The second one's longer, which is OK if you're not a distance runner. But if you're training for long distance, Morton's foot can cause a lot of problems. Backs, knees, ankles, everything can act up when you have Morton's foot."

Maureen was dazed. What did this mean then for her future as a runner, for her chance at the marathon?

"Now, first thing you'll have to do," the doctor continued, "is give that knee some rest. And I mean rest. We're going to put an elastic bandage on it to make sure you stay off it. When it starts feeling better, we'll see about some special orthotics for your shoes. That might help."

"Orth-what?"

"Orthotics. Something we put in your shoes to redistribute the weight so there's not so much pressure on your knees."

"Will that help?" Maureen asked faintly.

"It might. Can't guarantee anything, though. If the orthotics don't work, we'll have to play it by ear. We haven't had much experience with these stress injuries, but we're learning more all the time. It won't be long now. In ten years we'll be able to do all kinds of things."

Ten years! How about ten days! She'd start losing her conditioning after only a few days of inactivity. It wouldn't be long before she'd be back where she started: practically a Sunday jogger. Maureen was already beyond tears. She just stared silently at the floor as her mother wheeled her down the hall.

Back in the examining room, two interns started wrapping the elastic strips tightly around her bent leg. As they finished, they handed her two crutches, and she hobbled out the door, her hopes crushed.

Twelve

For three solid days Maureen watched TV. It didn't matter what—old cartoons, cooking shows, soaps. Anything would do. Once she sat through *Sesame Street* twice rather than struggle up to change the channel. The first time it was actually sort of funny. The Muppets had some great rock routines. The only time she moved was to go to bed—clutching the banister to hop up at night and slowly hobbling down again in the morning. In between she just sat, expressionless, staring at the tube.

Mrs. Meyer placed a bowl of tuna salad in front of her on a folding TV tray, then sat down beside her on the couch. "Here you are, honey. Try to eat a little more tonight, OK?"

"I'm not hungry, Mom."

"I know, but please, just a few bites."

Maureen picked up the fork and poked at the pieces of tuna and macaroni on her dish. She took a bite, but the tuna seemed dry and tasteless, the pasta heavy, and the lettuce limp. All in all, it looked the way she felt. She took another bite and managed to swallow it but almost gagged on the third.

Her mother watched helplessly as Maureen pushed the plate away.

"I can't, Mom. I just can't. I'll drink a glass of milk, but that's all I can manage."

Nagging didn't help, but neither did sympathy, suggestions of things to do, or stern threats of disaster if Maureen didn't pull herself together. Mrs. Meyer had tried everything, but Maureen was tuned out. She was a failure, pure and simple. In fact, she'd failed twice now—first with Jake and second with the marathon. She'd fallen short of her goals and lost her dreams.

The doorbell turned their attention away from the half-eaten dinner. Mrs. Meyer answered it and returned Maureen's dishes to the kitchen. It was Debbie, bringing over the day's assignments. She was delivering Maureen's homework and picking up her completed assignments for her classes.

"You'll have a snack, won't you, Debbie?" Mrs. Meyer called out from the kitchen.

"Of course."

She brought out a bowl of fresh fruit, and Debbie immediately helped herself. Maureen absentmindedly picked at the grapes while Debbie went over the assignments: twenty math problems, read chapter five in *A Tale of Two Cities*; review irregular verbs for a quiz in French on Monday.

"You *will* be back by Monday, won't you, Mo?"

"I don't know. I guess I'll be able to hobble around by then," she said despondently. "Can't sit home forever."

"Well, I hope so. We all really miss you at lunch, and I've been late almost every day this week without you to stop by and get me out of the house on time. You know, Mo, you'll feel ten times better when you start doing things again. Even going back to school will be better than sitting here like a lump all day."

A low "maybe" was Maureen's unenthusiastic response.

"I promise you, Debbie, she'll be back on Monday if I have to pull her there in a wagon," Mrs. Meyer announced as she stood in the doorway.

"Good. See you all *soon*," Debbie said pointedly as she got up to leave.

"Thanks for collecting all those assignments for Maureen. I know it must take a lot of your time."

"That's OK. I don't mind."

The next day Maureen returned to the doctor to have the bandage removed. Her knee was stiff, and the skin under the tight wrap was a pasty white. She could walk a little, if she was careful—but she didn't completely trust that knee. She clutched the banister and leaned on one crutch as she descended to the street. The doctor's advice was, "Wait and see," and she had a sheet of exercises from the physical therapist to do while she waited.

As they approached the front door, Maureen noticed a flat package, wrapped in white tissue paper and tied with a ribbon, stuck behind the screen door. It felt warm to the touch. As she opened the package, the aroma of Far Eastern spices filled the air. "It must be from Trang," she cried, brightening a little. Nestled inside a foil-lined box were a dozen pillow-shaped Vietnamese "ravioli."

The accompanying hand-printed note read: "Dear Maureen, I sorry you sick. Please, better soon. I miss the English lesson very much. Your friend, Trang."

Maureen's appetite suddenly returned. She devoured the entire contents of the box in a few minutes and was still hungry.

"I think this is a good sign," her mother said, laughing. "But I wish you'd saved me at least one."

"Sorry, Mom. I couldn't help it. All of a sudden I was famished."

No one really knew how she felt except her dad. He had called that day to say she had better put on her prettiest outfit because he was coming straight over to take her to lunch.

They went to Chef Wong's House, the best place in town. Maureen soon discovered, however, that trying to navigate a Chinese restaurant on crutches was next to impossible. The tables were too close together, and the booths for two were way in the back. But after her crutch nearly tripped a waiter who was carrying a huge platter of sizzling shrimp, the others gave her room to maneuver.

Maureen and her father settled into a booth and began to look at the big red menu. It was so hard to choose. They sat for a while before ordering, watching the dishes go by from the kitchen, finally deciding to try one destined for the next table that looked tempting. Twice-cooked pork, the waiter call it. She wondered why they had to cook it twice.

Mr. Meyer looked at her, brown eyes kind under shaggy brows. "Still glum, honey?"

"Oh, Dad, it's this dumb knee! I can't stand it!" Maureen burst out. She looked around the room, suddenly conscious of her loud voice. "I was getting really *good*," she continued in a softer tone. "You should've seen how I ran those hills. It was such a terrific feeling running past everyone. They'd be huffing and puffing, and I wouldn't even be breathing hard. Now I'm washed up—before my first race, even. It's not fair."

"Now, honey, don't talk like that. The knee will get better. Athletes have injuries, but they survive. They get back into shape and go on. You can do it, too. Your most important job is to give that knee the rest it needs. When it's better, you'll run again. I promise you will."

"Daddy, how can you promise? They don't even know for sure what's wrong. Maybe it won't get better. Maybe it'll keep giving out whenever I race."

"Then maybe you shouldn't be putting so much of yourself into racing. There *are* other things in life, you know."

"But, Dad, *you* always told me to work hard, aim high, and not let anything get in my way. That's what I was doing. I feel so cheated."

Her father sighed. "You're right. I did tell you that, and it is important to do your best and be the best. But I guess I forgot to tell you something else just as important. Remember the 'Golden Mean'? It means the middle way. The ancient Greeks thought to be happy you should avoid extremes. It sounds to me as though you've been pushing yourself too hard, and now you're going to have to stop and head back toward the middle of the road." Mr. Meyer paused for a moment, studying his daughter's face. "Don't you think so?"

"All I know is I wanted something very badly," Maureen replied hesitantly. "I put everything I had into it, and now it looks as if I can't have it because I wanted it too much. That's not fair."

They ate the rest of their meal in silence. Maureen had hoped for sympathy, not a lecture, and she couldn't understand why her father wasn't more understanding.

The next day, Maureen went through the motions of going to school, but her heart wasn't in it. She felt ridiculous limping around on the crutches and didn't care if she passed or failed her courses. Several times she caught a glimpse of Jake in the halls, which was unusual, but she never looked over at him or waved. The last thing she needed was his sympathy. She didn't want Jake, of all people, to feel sorry for her.

Debbie found she had to do a lot more than her share of keeping up the conversation at lunch. Luckily, she had saved up quite a few things to say during the weeks when Maureen had been devoting herself to running and didn't seem to mind her friend's lack of participation.

Soon Maureen didn't need the crutches anymore, but her knee still ached when she walked and hurt unbearably when she tried to run a few steps. She was getting custom-molded insoles for her shoes that cost over a hundred dollars. Her dad had come through with the money for that. He knew how important it was for her to keep trying. But the doctor still seemed so vague about when she might run again that she didn't know what to think. She felt immobilized. Burned out.

It doesn't matter when I can run again, Maureen told herself. *Nothing matters anymore at all.*

Thirteen

Maureen had just started listening to an old blues record she'd borrowed from Debbie's collection when the phone rang. She liked listening to the blues when she was feeling low. The songs were mostly about disaster—lost love, hard times, even death, but they had a feeling of hope, with an underlying humor that usually cheered Maureen up a little. Maybe it helped to know that there were people who had it a lot worse than she did, but that they "kept on truckin'."

Lost love. It must be pretty common, she thought as she limped over to get the phone. There were so many songs about it. Well, she knew how that felt. Now she'd lost her only goal in life, too. She was a two-time loser.

Picking up the phone, she could hardly believe her ears. It was Jake, and he wanted to see her!

"Maureen, hi. I'm glad you're home. Look, I

have something I want to show you. Can I come over in about fifteen minutes?"

Stunned, Maureen took a moment to find her voice. "Sure. What is it?"

"You'll see. Be right over."

She couldn't imagine what Jake wanted. What could he possibly have to show her? She wondered if it was worth struggling upstairs to comb her hair. Her knee still complained on the stairs with a sharp jab every time her weight shifted. She sat on the couch, her hand still resting on the phone, thinking it over. *If you can't walk, you ought to at least have nice hair,* she thought. *Too late now—there's the doorbell already.*

"Hi, Mo!" Jake stood on her doorstep, a big smile on his face. Dressed in jeans and a T-shirt, he looked achingly familiar. He was holding a large leather case.

"That was fast. Come on in the kitchen. I'll get us something cold to drink."

"OK. I'll lay these out on the table. I can't wait for you to see them!" Jake paused. "Um, Maureen, I'm really sorry about your leg—or whatever it was that happened to prevent you from running."

Maureen just shrugged. She didn't want to start crying in front of Jake.

"I seemed to see you running everywhere I went," Jake continued. "That's how I got the idea for this portfolio. I hope seeing these doesn't make you feel worse."

"I couldn't feel much worse," Maureen admitted.

"I've been in the darkroom pretty steadily for the last two weeks trying to get these prints perfect. The *Gazette* wants to print them in a feature article on Boston runners in the Sunday magazine. I hope you don't mind signing a model's release. They might want to interview you, too." Jake opened his case while he talked and laid the prints out on the table. He stood there, bending over the photos.

Maureen gasped. "That's me! They're all pictures of me! When did you take these? I never noticed you taking them. How did you do it?"

"I have a telephoto lens. I never get too close to my subjects. It makes them self-conscious. With this lens I can get close-ups from quite a distance away."

"I can't believe you did it. I never suspected. They're beautiful, Jake," she added as her shock and amazement subsided and pride set in. "Really beautiful! I mean . . . the prints. I didn't know you were so good. I mean . . ."

"That's OK. I know what you mean. I work hard at it. I've sold a lot of pictures to the *Gazette*, but this is the first time they've taken a whole series." Jake laughed, a note of pride in his voice.

Each picture had life. The lines were strong, the contrast sharp. And each one caught some of the feelings experienced by a runner: the exhilaration, the pain, the beauty of a perfect day, the exhaustion.

In the first one she was stretching out, her leg going back to form a wide angle with the one bent under her body. Her thin arms were reaching up to the trunk of a tree, its dark, rough texture contrasting with her smooth, light skin.

In another she was smiling, an exuberant, self-satisfied smile, while a brilliant sun reflected every detail of the surrounding trees and flowers in the pond behind her. She remembered that day. She was flying, beating all of her previous times for that run.

There was one taken in the rain—all shades of gray—her hair sticking wet to her cheeks, a drop of water on the tip of her chin, T-shirt clinging to her slim body . . .

The one she liked best was of her running through a circle of sprinklers at the park. Small faces looked up in amazement as she ran through. She remembered one well-trained tot who'd scolded her for going in with her shoes on.

The last one in the series was on Heartbreak Hill. This one was filled with agony. Her mouth was twisted in pain. Sweat poured down her face. Her leg muscles were straining. She wondered if that was taken on her last day. She'd run it so many times, they were blurred together in her memory.

"Do you really like them?" Jake asked anxiously. "I took a lot of other runners for this project, too, but I liked the ones of you best. I hope you do, too, and that you don't mind my having followed you around so much," he finished awkwardly.

"I love them, Jake," Maureen whispered, overwhelmed. "They're great. They really show what it's like, the bad with the good. I didn't think a picture could ever show so much movement and feeling."

His hand rested on her shoulder as they bent over the photos. "I'm really glad you like them. I worked night and day on these, and I think they're the best stuff I've ever done."

Maureen sighed. Jake squeezed her shoulder. "Mo, don't be sad. I know you'll be able to run again. A bad knee can't keep you down."

"I don't know." She shrugged. "If I knew what was wrong with it, I could fight. But nobody has any answers. 'Just rest. Wait and see.' That's all I have to go on."

"Mo, you're going to run. You'll be a good runner, maybe a great one. But you can't do it all at once, and you can't do it by yourself. You don't even have a coach. It took me five or six years to learn how to get photos like these, and I had a lot of help . . . good teachers, pointers from other photographers . . . And I made a lot of mistakes, too. Wasted a lot of time doing things over. Now you're going to have to start over. But it won't be like going back to the very beginning. You'll be a lot smarter. You'll know not to do too much too soon."

Maureen was starting to believe it. Maybe there was hope—not only for her future as a runner, but for her future with Jake as well.

Jake put his hands on her shoulders, and turned her toward him, and shyly, hopefully, they looked into each other's eyes. "No more brotherly advice . . . I love you."

He kissed her before she could answer. All her feelings of frustration and anger and loss faded away as she felt Jake's warm arms around her. Pulling away for a second, Jake looked at her tenderly before his lips met hers and they kissed again. Maureen felt as if the sun had suddenly come out—she had been living under dark clouds for too long. Now anything seemed possible. Love could brighten the darkest day, lift the deepest despair.

Her arms circled his back, and she held him tightly. She wouldn't let him get away now. What a feeling! She loved being in Jake's arms and feeling her arms around him, knowing he loved her and believed in her.

It really *didn't* matter that he couldn't run with her. He understood how she felt; she could see that from the pictures. That was what was important.

Jake gave her one last kiss on the forehead, and they went into the living room and sat down on the couch. "I'm glad we've finally gotten together. I'm just sorry you had to get hurt before we came to our senses."

"What do you mean?" Maureen asked.

"Well, I thought it couldn't work out between us because of your running. You were so obsessed with training, and I thought you wouldn't have been happy with anyone who wasn't a runner. There was nothing for me to do if I couldn't run with you. I wouldn't have fit into your life very well. At least that was how I felt," Jake said.

"So I wrote off our relationship, but I kept pursuing you as a photographic subject. I loved taking those pictures of you, and through my camera I really got into your running. When you got hurt and began limping around school, I was almost as disappointed as you. More than disappointed," Jake went on. "All at once I realized something: that I loved your running and missed it because it was all a part of who you were. I don't want you interested in something else, because then you wouldn't be my Maureen. I'm just sorry I let my stupid pride get in

177

the way for so long," he finished, holding her hands.

Maureen didn't know whether to laugh or to cry. She felt so happy and whole again. Jake's words had touched something deep inside, though, and she had something to say, too.

"You don't know how much that means to me. You're a very talented and special person. And I've definitely had my blind spots, as well. I was too closed off, not ready to understand your special interests. I think I was trying to prove something to myself, and I shut out everyone else. Maybe this injury has done me some good, after all. It's forced me to slow down long enough to see how silly I was to have such a one-track mind. We can still enjoy a lot of things together, can't we?"

Jake ran his fingers through her curls. "You bet," he said softly. "Now, how about that cold drink? You know, I hardly *ever* do this much serious talking."

"Me neither. Hope you like Tab. That's all we have around here."

They finished their sodas nestled comfortably on the couch. Then Jake looked at his watch.

"Got to run," he said abruptly. "I've got a deadline." He jumped up and started replacing the prints in his portfolio. "I've got to get these downtown by five o'clock. I just wanted you to see them first."

Maureen stood up and took his hand in hers as they walked toward the door.

"Hope you don't have any plans for tomorrow afternoon," Jake said.

"Not anymore."

"Good! I'm going to take you for a walk. We've got to get that knee working again, and I'm going to see that you don't overdo it. We've got a lot of talking to do, and this time I don't want to get out of breath."

"OK. See you tomorrow."

When Mrs. Meyer came home, she heard Maureen singing upstairs. She went up and looked into Maureen's room to find her daughter actually smiling as she repeated the ritual of going through her closet.

"Maureen! What's going on here? Something wonderful must have happened. You look like a new person!"

"Oh, Mom, something wonderful *did* happen. I'm in love!"

"Prince Charming must have been here, then. Where is he? I want to meet him." She looked around for a tall, dark, handsome stranger.

"Mom, you *did* meet him. You know. It's *Jake*. Remember?"

"Well, yes. I do remember. He did seem pretty charming, actually. But I thought you had given up on boys. Haven't seen any around here lately."

"Well, I had. I was discouraged. I never seemed

to do the right thing, and I thought Jake liked someone else. But I was wrong. He liked me, but I was so busy running I couldn't see it."

"I know. Your training schedule didn't leave much time for people. I was even beginning to miss you. We all were."

"You know what, Mom? All the time I was training, Jake was taking pictures of me running, and I didn't even notice! I used to see him a lot going around with his camera and that big bag of lenses, but I never suspected he was taking shots of me. I still can't believe it."

"Well, you are very photogenic."

"The prints are great, Mom. Not because of me, but because he really showed what it's like when you run. He really understands it. And he's going to help me start running again."

The phone interrupted their conversation.

"It's Debbie!" her mother said.

"Thanks, I'll come out and bring it back in here."

"Maureen! Where have you been? You were supposed to meet me at the library this afternoon."

"Oh, no! I'm really sorry. I forgot all about it. Jake came over, and it sort of knocked everything else right out of my mind."

"Well, I guess that's a pretty good excuse. What happened?"

"Well, Deb, you were right all along. Two people don't always have to do the same things when they're in love. That could get pretty boring. It's sharing and understanding each other's feelings that count."

"Can I say 'I told you so'?"

"Jake's even going to help me start running again. I've got it all figured out—how I'll build up my knee gradually, then I'll enter some qualifying races in the fall and maybe the marathon next spring."

"But how can Jake help you run? He doesn't know the first thing about it."

"I know, but it's really just moral support that I need—someone who believes in me. It's hard for two runners to train together, anyway. They are always at different stages and need to do different things. It can get pretty competitive, too."

"Wow, you really have big plans all of a sudden. Sounds terrific. I can hardly believe it, though. Everything happened so fast!"

"It sure did. These last few weeks have been the worst in my life, and I'm glad they're over. I never want to feel that bad again."

"Well, you sound great now—you're your old self again."

"Hey, Debbie, do you think your parents would let you have another party soon? I think I'd have a lot more fun at the next one. I wouldn't let Karen take him away from me this time."

"You're learning fast, kid! But I'm not the only one who can have parties, you know. Why don't you have one?"

Maureen thought a moment. "It's true, I could, and will—soon. But I don't think I can go quite that fast yet. I have a lot of catching up to do. I have a boyfriend, but I still haven't had my first date. We're going for a walk tomorrow, but I hope he'll ask me to a movie this weekend."

Debbie laughed. "Sounds like fun. Don't overdo it on the buttered popcorn, though. Now that you're not running fifty miles a week anymore, you'll have to eat the way the rest of us do—every bite counts."

"Oh, don't remind me. My diet starts tomorrow. You know, this is really terrible! I've never had to go on a diet before. Three weeks of not running has taken me right to fat city."

"Aha! At last you know what it's like! Hmmm, I didn't realize that's how you stayed so thin. Do you think I could start running, too? It would be worth it if I could have a little ice cream sundae once in a while. How about it, Mo? I won't hang around you and Jake too much; just give me a few pointers to get started. OK?"

"Gee, Debbie, I've been trying to get you to run with me for ages. I didn't know the secret to winning you over was free calories."

"Of course. I'd do anything for ice cream. You just never put it quite that way before."

"I have an idea. Let's ask Trang if she wants to run with us, too. We can all start off really easily together in the beginning. Then you two can run together when I start serious training again."

"Okay. Before we start, though, I think I'll have to make a little trip out to Bloomingdale's."

"Debbie, you don't need a designer running suit! Just wear a pair of old shorts and a T-shirt."

"Maureen, you *really do* have a lot to learn! There's a prom coming up this month, and I don't know about you, but I have *not* been invited yet. You can't be too careful, you know. I have to be seen at my best at all times."

"I've got to hand it to you, Debbie. You really are a pro."

The next afternoon Jake and Maureen walked for a couple of miles, stopping in the neighborhood parks to rest when her knee began to tire. They climbed on the horse swings at one playground and lazily pumped back and forth, giggling at the sight of the poor ponies and their oversize loads. At the next rest stop, Jake pulled her up into a large willow tree, which had been split apart in the last big storm.

They sat with their backs propped against

the upper branches staring into the leaf-laced sky.

When they walked again they went to a little nature sanctuary, tucked away behind some tennis courts. Maureen had never known the place even existed. It was fenced off from the rest of the park, and a faded sign on the gate warned everyone who came in to leave the area exactly as they had found it.

It was wonderfully quiet and serene. They followed the path around the pond, single-file, listening to the birds and the crunch of sticks and leaves underfoot. A low wooden dock extended out from the woods over a marshy area. Jake led Maureen to the end, and they lay down on the weathered boards. Maureen rested her chin on her folded arms and looked out into the pond. Turtles were sunning on a log not far away, and pretty soon a duck swam up to them. They remained still, lying in silence for a while, listening to the small sounds, smelling the musty boards beneath their bare arms and the swamp grasses below.

Maureen turned her head and looked at Jake and saw that he was looking at her. He smiled and started to say something, but she reached over to touch his lips. She didn't want to interrupt the perfect quiet beauty of the moment. She felt his hand slide lightly around her shoulder, and he leaned toward her, kissing her forehead, then her nose, and finally her lips.

Thrilled at his touch, Maureen felt as if she were melting into the boards beneath her. The gentle sound of the water lapping below, the warmth of Jake lying next to her, and the fresh earthy smells of June made her heart soar with joy. Being in love was wonderful. She knew this was the beginning of something very special— something that would last a long, long time.

The kiss ended abruptly, however, with giggles from the shore. A group of cub scouts, notebooks and pencils in hand, yellow scarves neatly tied over blue, badge-covered shirts, stood snickering at the end of the path.

"Excuse us, please," the woman who was their leader whispered. "We have come to observe the ducks."

Maureen and Jake hopped up, arms entwined, and continued on their way, hardly noticing the confusion they left behind them.

As they continued along the nature trail, Maureen remembered the day they had met. It seemed ages ago.

"Jake, remember that picture I took of you? At the marathon? How'd it come out, anyway?"

"Well, Maureen, let me put it this way. You stick to running, I'll stick to photography, and we'll make a pretty good team."